DREAMS NEVERSEEN

BELLA AND THE BEAST MASTER
BOOK THREE

SARAH WESTILL

DREAMS NEVER SEEN

Bella and the Beast Master – Book Three

Copyright 2023 by Sarah Westill

ISBN 978-1-955293-21-1

Cover Design by For the Muse Designs

OTHER TITLES BY SARAH WESTILL

GEN-HEIRS: The Guardians of Sziveria

(in reading order)

Levkaseon – A Prequel

Wintersfall

Raiventon

Kynhaven

Asherwick

Ericksen - A Wintervail Special

Survaine

Wolvenguard (Nov. 29th 2023)

Bella and the Beast Master

Gen-Heirs world series

Frozen Flowers Fallen

Perfect Melody Silenced

Dreams Never Seen

Fiery Nights Tempted (Feb. 14th 2024)

For world maps be sure to visit www.sarahwestill.com

To get the latest updates, follow Sarah on Instagram
@authorsarahwestill

DEDICATION

Huge thank you to Julie and Nikita, who braved this story before anyone else! You both are so amazing and I'm thankful to have you on my writing journey.

CONTENT WARNING:
This book contains mature content
Reader discretion is advised.

CHAPTER

ONE

HAVEN CITY, SZIVERIA
March, 25th 802 P.C.E. (post-cataclysmic event)

BELLA RALSTON STOMPED her boots on the thick snow covering the sidewalk. She tried to convince herself the action was to keep warm, but nothing short of a fire would manage that feat. Nerves and excitement left her too antsy to stand still. Pedestrians split in a sea of travelers around her, some arriving at the MagnaRail station, others heading out of the city.

Like a handful of others, Bella had opted to wait for her arrival outside the station instead of within, where she'd not only have to contend with passengers but vendors and pickpockets. Out on the sidewalk was a little calmer. Not exactly how she would have chosen to greet her husband after six months apart.

Markus had booked passage on the first ship daring enough to venture the Northern Pass before the ice flows had completely stopped. There was a high risk involved, hitting an iceberg a real threat, but Markus had decided to take the chance. Bella had spent the last week waking up screaming, drenched in a cold sweat, convinced her husband was frozen at the bottom of the Black Ocean. If all had gone according to plan, he'd be stepping through those doors.

Any moment.

Her feet stomped harder. A shiver raced along her spine and trembled through every limb. Biting wind stung her nose and cheeks. She shoved her hands deeper into the pockets of her winter coat. Behind her, the horse attached to a carriage for hire neighed and stomped its displeasure.

"Will it be much longer, miss?" the driver called down.

Bella glanced over her shoulder. He struggled to calm the animal. She frowned and looked at the entryway to the station. "I don't know. If you need to leave, you can."

"Perhaps just around the block?" he inquired, a hopeful rise in his voice.

Bella forced her frozen lips into a smile. "That should be fine."

He tipped his hat. "Thank you, miss."

The driver had to wait until a bicyclist and two carriages went past before easing away from the shoulder and the other drivers waiting for fares. An Ariot attempted to zip around the slower boxy rides but was cut off by an oncoming carriage. The little vehicle, powered by a magnetically charged engine, swerved back onto the correct side of the road. Bella sighed. At times she wondered about the benefit of new technology.

Burrowing deeper into her jacket, she faced the constant flow of foot traffic and took a deep inhale of the ice-laden air. Oh summer sun, what if Markus had made a grave mistake traveling so early in the season? Her exhale surrounded her in a cloud of vapor.

A commotion broke out at the entrance and Bella's heart leaped into her throat. She rose on her tiptoes and tried to see over the crowd. The mass of people split in alarm, and a silver blur broke through.

Bella, my Bella!

Searing pain stabbed into Bella's mind. She cried out as her vision wavered, and the sidewalk seemed to buck under her feet. A familiar masculine voice roared her name, but the agony tearing through her head made it impossible for her to respond. Darkness pulled her under. Multiple, frantic noises filtered through the haze of unconsciousness and Bella sucked in a ragged breath.

"Bel... come ba..."

Be... so... be...

A man's voice faded in and out, fighting a more persistent presence in her mind. Both spouted incoherent phrases that made her head pound harder. She tried to wave the offending sounds away. Gradually, the sharp throbbing eased and her eyes fluttered open. Markus's beautiful golden eyes stared down at her. Concern pinched his handsome face and pressed his mouth into a firm line. A wet tongue licked her cheek and jaw. Bella turned her head and met

Lunah's anxious stare, so similar in color to her masters.

"Wha..." The word lodged in her throat, her tongue suddenly too large and dry to speak.

"Shh," Markus said, her fingers brushing along her brow to her temple. "Don't speak. Not yet."

That sounded like a fabulous plan. She closed her eyes again and focused on breathing. When the snow underneath her body began to melt and soak her clothes, Bella squirmed and attempted to speak once again. Markus helped her rise into a sitting position. Lunah laid her muzzle on Bella's thigh.

Pressing her fingers to her forehead, Bella asked, "What happened?"

Markus rubbed her back and held her hand. "Lunah was too excited and she forced your bond too fast."

Something thick dribbled from her nose. She blinked and touched her upper lip. Her fingertips came away bright with blood. Markus reached into his pocket and pulled out a handkerchief. He dabbed at her nose before she could take it from him.

"The driver behind me says he's been waiting for you? He said he wouldn't have left if he'd known you were sick," Markus said.

"His horse was cold," she said, the fog in her mind clearing until she became aware of all the people staring down at her, including the worried driver. Her first attempt to rise ended in Markus having to grab her waist to keep her from falling forward. The second time she managed and held her hands out. "I'm okay, I'm fine, I can stand on my own."

The doubt in his stare suggested he didn't believe a word she said. "Then let me hold onto your arm for myself. You scared a solid year off my life."

Bella allowed him to help her into the carriage. Inside the dim interior, she collapsed onto the wooden bench seat and closed her eyes.

"Bella? Bella!" Markus leaped into the cabin and grabbed her knee and shoulder.

Her eyes flew open and she stared at him. "I'm fine, it's okay."

"Keep your eyes open for me, please?" he asked, settling across from her, the seats too narrow for him to join her. Lunah lay on their feet.

"Where's your bag?" she asked.

"I have two chests. The driver handled them while you were recovering on the sidewalk."

Bella frowned and wiggled her toes underneath the wolf who'd been the reason she'd needed to *recover*. Then her gaze shifted over her husband. The fur-lined coat he wore added to his already substantial bulk. His long, dark braid draped over his shoulder. The windows in the carriage provided enough light to define the harsher angles of his face. His high cheekbones, full mouth, and deep-set eyes, all familiar and so beautiful to her.

"Hello," she whispered, offering a watery smile. He was really here, before her, back in Sziveria. Her heart swelled to bursting.

The carriage rocked into motion. He leaned

forward and took her hand in his, squeezing. "Hello, my mate."

"Not how I imagined our reunion going," she said, sighing.

He threaded their fingers together and leaned across enough to kiss her hand. "I, too, would have preferred something different."

"How long are you staying this time?" she asked, even though she feared the answer.

"I would rather not have this conversation in a carriage," he said, a sad smile of apology curving his lips.

Bella tugged her hand free and collapsed back on the seat. "That bad, huh?"

"Maybe," was all he said, rubbing his knuckles under his chin along the short bristles of his beard.

No, this was not how Bella imagined their first meeting as a married couple. She'd envisioned passion, excitement, and unrestrained longing that would occupy their journey home. Instead, they sat in uncomfortable silence, a shallow ache still buzzing in her head. Lunah whined on the floor.

"She is still very sorry," Markus murmured.

Bella crossed her arms over her chest and watched the city sliding past. Inhabitants were emerging from their homes after months indoors, braving the frigid temperatures for necessary supplies and to just get outside. Sidewalks and storefronts were packed. Street vendors would begin setting up in a few weeks when the worst of the snow and ice dissipated. They crossed over the river and the scenery changed to sprawling apartment buildings and affluent houses. The colorful, parklike shopping area known as Extilis Square passed by. Most of the retailers were still closed, except for Mr. Harold's Book Emporium, which opened the moment locals matriculated on the sidewalk. Bella often wondered if the owner had an apartment in the building no one knew about.

The carriage slowed and then stopped in front of the building Markus had purchased a brand-new apartment in almost six months ago. The reason he'd contracted with her, the dwelling couldn't remain vacant through the winter. Perhaps Bella should have reminded herself of that before she'd allowed her anticipation to get the best of her and lead to disappointment. They'd exchanged no words of love, though he had hinted at a future with her. One she'd clung to in the months when only a few quick radio calls had sustained the sense of a relationship.

The moment the door opened, Lunah hopped out and waited on the sidewalk. Midday sun glistened off the packed ice at her feet and glared white, making Bella squint. Markus helped her down and then hopped out after her. He paid their fare and accepted the two massive chests from the driver. Grabbing onto the leather handles on one end, he hefted one in each hand and that's when Bella noticed the little wheels on the other end.

"I've never seen that before," she said.

"You haven't traveled much," he replied, grinning. The dimples that made her breath hitch popped out on either side of his mouth. "I wouldn't recommend carting a large amount of belongings any other way."

Her breath caught for an entirely new reason. "You... have a lot of things?"

"What I needed until the rest of my belongings can ship once the ice flows are finished. My cousin will handle that when it's time."

She grabbed one of the many glass doors along the front of the building and stood off to the side. Warm, moist air teased her hair. The rich scent of earth and healthy plants competed with the icy drafts racing by. He pulled one trunk, then another, through the entry. Lunah followed and Bella let the door swing shut. Tenants meandered along the trails winding through the greenhouse. Baby dwarf trees and potted plants thrived in the temperate climate. Years from now, the conservatory would brim with greenery as everything grew.

At the stairwell, she held the door once again. The cases banged and bumped up the cement stairs, drowning out Bella's booted steps and Lunah's claws. They reached the seventh floor and Markus used his hip to force the door open. He shoved one box through, then the other. Bella raised a brow and paused on the landing, her hand braced on the rail.

"What is—" She didn't get the chance to finish her question. He moved faster than she could track, snatching her to his chest, his mouth crashing to hers in a searing kiss.

No hesitation. Bella opened her mouth, moaning as his tongue slid along hers. Deep in the night she'd often wondered if she imagined his intoxicating taste. If the brief moment of passion she'd experienced at his touch had been nothing more than a fabrication of her lonely mind. He stumbled them into the nearest wall, his body caging hers in, and Bella knew the memories were all too real. Heat flared within her. Too many layers were between them, cushioning his solid frame as he pressed close.

"Summer sun, I missed you." He kissed the corner of her mouth, her chin, her jaw, and down along her throat.

Desire curled her toes and his words loosened the anxiety that maybe, just maybe, she'd had everything wrong concerning their relationship. He didn't give her the chance to respond, claiming her mouth again for another intense kiss. They both fumbled with the buttons of each other's jackets, their fingers tangling together. And still, he kissed her, his mouth slanting over hers, devouring like he'd been starving for her. A desperate need surged at her center until she clawed at his clothing, hating every barrier keeping her from touching his bare skin. Stars above, she *needed* him.

One hand on her rear, the other around her waist, wedging her questing hands between them, he dragged her hips to his and staggered them closer to their apartment. Bella's breath sawed from her lungs, and despite being trapped, she still managed to separate the edges of his coat and yank his sweater and undershirt up enough to touch his flanks. A tremble raced through them both. Her back slammed into another wall and he lifted her thigh, anchoring it to his, fitting into the cradle he'd created between her legs. His hips surged forward, the hard length of his erection grinding against her in the perfect spot. Pleasure exploded at her core. She cried out, her nails digging into his sides.

Smooth skin and muscles flexed beneath her fingers, but she wanted more, and apparently, Markus did too. He shifted enough space between them to shove a hand beneath her shirt and—

A masculine voice cleared. Multiple times. "Oh dear, um, hello?"

Bella and Markus froze. At the same time, they turned their heads and stared at the intruder. Half hidden in their recessed doorway, a man stared at them with big eyes behind glasses set into thick, black frames. Red stained his entire face and he fiddled with one of the large buttons on his black peacoat. Dark brown curls were a chaotic mess around his head. The pencil mustache over his tense mouth twitched.

Slowly, Markus eased his hand out from under her clothes and she did the same, though he didn't otherwise move. Bella let her leg drop from his hold.

"May we help you?" Markus asked.

The stranger cleared his throat and brought a bulging messenger bag to his chest, hugging the leather. "I was told to see you about a job."

Markus pointed first at himself, then at Bella. "Me, or..."

Her disappointment at being interrupted kept her from slapping his chest. Why would anyone ever want to see her about something?

She was a file clerk. Unless they were hoping to bribe her into allowing them into long-term storage, she had nothing much to offer. And even that would be a solid *no*. Her job may be menial, but she still took pride in her work.

"You," the man said before Markus could finish. "Markus Ralston?"

Markus sighed and stepped away from her. Bella had to fist her hands to keep from grabbing and pulling him back, the loss an ache in her chest.

"Yes, I'm Markus." He muttered under his breath. "Will you please see our guest inside while I get my things?"

Lunah whined and Markus spoke to her in Ruthenian. She yipped and lowered her front paws to the floor. Bella edged past their visitor, offering an uncomfortable smile. She pulled the apartment key from her jacket pocket and opened the door. Warm noon sun brightened the living room, streaming in from the wall of windows overlooking the city. The butter-yellow walls and cream carpet created an inviting space, no matter the season.

Bella beckoned the man to enter, not surprised when his eyes widened further at the empty room. Only a dining table visible through the wide arches and a rug in front of the woodstove indicated anyone even lived in the spacious residence.

"We moved in right before winter," Bella said by way of excuse. "Haven't had a chance to get furniture."

She'd refused to bring the worn and tattered

couch and end tables from her and her mother's old home, and buying furniture without Markus, when he'd bought the apartment, seemed wrong.

Markus's chests banged against the door-frame. He shoved one, then the other, into the living room. Lunah trotted by and started investigating every surface, disappearing down the hall to the left. The guest went into the dining area and set his bag on the table. Markus used his foot to close the door, and then, fists on his hips, he stared at the bare room.

Confusion, disappointment, and finally resignation flickered across his handsome face. The warm reflection of light gave his already caramel skin a richer hue. Bella's heart skipped and she found herself before him without realizing she'd even begun to move. His rough fingers threaded through hers and he pulled her close.

"Why?" he whispered.

Bella didn't pretend not to know what he was asking. She brought their joined hands to her chest and held tight. "Because you weren't here."

He brushed a curl from her temple and leaned close... A throat cleared. Markus rested his forehead on hers, sighing.

"I have just arrived in your country." He lifted his head and Bella followed his gaze to their guest standing at the table. "How did you know I'd be here?"

The flustered man fiddled with the collar of the white shirt he wore under his coat. "A Mr. Benirak? He said I could find you here today."

Bella turned. "Arch Guardian Wolvenguard?"

The man choked. "A-arch g-guardian? No...

no, he was at the museum helping our curator unbox art pieces on loan from Ruthenia. She asked Immigration and Import if they knew anyone who could help translate when the shipment arrived and they recommended Mr. Benirak."

"Nicolas Benirak *is* the arch guardian of Wolvenguard," Markus stated.

The man took off his glasses and polished the lenses using his jacket sleeve. "Oh my, an arch guardian..."

"I'm going to punch Nick the next time I see him," Markus muttered.

"You work at the museum?" Bella asked, wanting to get whatever this man needed handled so she could finally spend time with her husband. Or she could beat Markus to punching Nick. She knew where the arch guardian resided.

"Oh yes, so sorry, where is my etiquette?" He popped his glasses back on his face and wiped his hands on his pants, and then held out his palm. "Leander Kavont, I'm the assistant director of ancient civilizations at the Sziverian Museum for History and Arts."

Markus shook his hand. "Why did Nick send you to me?"

Leander sucked in a breath and rubbed his hands on the front of his pants again. "A dear friend of mine is missing." He exhaled heavily and looked between the two of them, worry pinching his forehead. "In Thanzia."

Confused, Bella glanced at Markus before directing her attention back to Leander. "Why would you need my husband's help for something in another country, Mr. Kavont?"

"I-I'm afraid that it's all rather complicated," he said, a fine sheen of sweat coating his face. "But I'll do my best to explain what I know."

"Can you return tomorrow?" Markus asked.

Leander fumbled with the clasps holding his stuffed bag together. "Well, see, that's the problem." The brass latches clanged against the table as the satchel flopped open. Papers crinkled and slid as he searched inside. "I have a... where is it, I know I stuffed it in here, ah yes, here we go. I have a schedule for departures to Thanzia, and the first ship for the season leaves Friday at dawn. If we catch the next MagnaRail to Port Anchor, we can be there in time to make boarding. Another ship doesn't go to Thanzia for almost six weeks."

Leander held out the paper, shaking it slightly in her direction. "See?"

Bella accepted the schedule, unsure what he expected her to do with it though. "And six weeks would be too long?"

"Yes! Far too long," he said, a breath of relief rushing from him. "I'm so glad you understand."

Markus took the schedule from her and sat in the nearest chair hard enough to make the spindle legs groan. He tossed the paper into the middle of the table. "Why don't you explain what is going on."

Leander dug around inside his bag again. Papers fluttered to the floor and slid across the surface. He made a small stack off to the side, ignoring the pages he didn't seem to need. Bella crouched down and gathered them together.

"Three weeks ago, Oberon Rima, an archaeologist I work closely with for acquisitions for the museum, sent me the most exciting letter. He asked me to radio him at my first opportunity and I did. By then, he'd made even more discoveries. I told my director about Oberon's findings and he said if they were legitimate, the museum would help fund the discovery." He pushed his glasses up on his nose. "We help fund many historically significant finds."

"And ensure the Sziverian Museum for History and Art gets the first choice of artifacts or culturally significant works," Bella said, smiling.

"We work closely with many other museums in the inhabited world," he said, lifting his chin.

"I'm a long-time visitor of the art wing. I'm very aware of how many countries the museum partners with," Bella said, staying calm. No doubt Leander had had to defend the institution's business model many times.

"Yes, well." Leander sorted through papers in his hands. "A museum isn't much of a showcase of humanity without a variety of the human spirit. I am very proud of our diverse selection and the history we can share. Oberon's discovery, if legitimate, will be the find of our generation."

Markus held his hands open. "Why don't you start at the beginning."

"Yes, of course." Leander smoothed a hand down his coat and took a seat across from Markus. He looked down at the papers in his hand, startled as if surprised he still held them and then shoved the bunch at her husband. "This is his letter. To me."

Taking the missive, Markus flipped through the pages. "He found the remains of a pre-cataclysmic city?"

Leander nodded, his mop of curls bouncing. "Yes. Just like the ones off our coast, remnants of steel and glass. Roads made of some black substance. Huge metal vehicles. All of it so amazing, so..." He threw his hands into the air. "Unreal! To think we once had so many resources we could build into the sky as far as we could see! Of course, all we have is a few stories and paintings to show we once existed as such. But to find the proof in the ground? No denying."

"Many would wish to steal the ruins for those very resources. Many of our rails in Ruthenia are used from recovered steel, still viable even after hundreds of years. A city's worth?" Markus tsked. "He might as well have found a horde of gold."

"I am very concerned about the find for multiple reasons. But my biggest worry is my friend." Leander looked between them, his pencil mustache twitching over his frown. "He has gone missing."

CHAPTER

TWO

By some great feat, Markus didn't bang his head on the table in sheer frustration. *Of course,* the archaeologist friend was missing. *Of course,* there was a legitimate emergency keeping Markus from claiming his mate. Whom he'd waited six long months to see, to touch, to love. To speak to in person and begin living life together. Markus spread his hands over the smooth surface of the table and forced a sense of calm he didn't feel.

"How do you know he's missing?" Markus asked.

"He answered my radio calls every time until last week. When I inquired with the Thanzia Institute of Culture, where he works, they said he hadn't been heard from for eight days," Leander answered. He stacked his hands on the table and leaned forward. "I'm very worried he's either been kidnapped for information about the dig from a rival researcher, or he's been murdered by looters."

"Or killed by the rivals," Bella said, moving a

seat to sit next to Markus. "If he had yet to take credit..."

Leander tapped on the table. "Yes, that is my concern, too. I need to learn what might have happened, and I can't do that from here."

"Why do you need my husband to do that?" Bella picked up the letter and looked over the pages.

"The museum has given me permission to travel to Thanzia, but because of the possible danger, I can't go alone." Leander fiddled with a brass buckle, making the little clasp rattle on the table. "I asked two enforcement and four reward seekers. They all turned me down. No one is willing to leave the country. When Mr. Benirak, um, rather, the arch guardian overheard me talking to our curator about my dilemma, he recommended you, Mr. Ralston."

An apologetic smile crossed Leander's face and he held his hands open. "So, you see, you're my last resort. If you say no, history itself could be lost to us."

"Give me a moment with my wife, please," Markus requested, taking Bella's hand and rising.

Leander rose when Bella did. "Yes, please, whatever you need."

Markus pulled Bella across the apartment, down a short hall off the living room, and into their... bedroom? He stopped so fast she slammed into his back. The only furniture in the room was a large bed with a bare mattress. No dressers, nightstands, or chests. A bare wood floor and barren walls made the unused bed even more obvious. Markus hadn't known what to expect when he arrived in the home he'd share with Bella. An empty shell hadn't crossed his mind, however. So many nights spent alone, without her, he'd imagined how she'd been making their space. What she'd choose, what colors, and if he'd like them. And even if the colors wouldn't have agreed with him, he'd have loved them because they were *her*. His Bella.

"Have you even been living here?" he asked, unable to keep the hurt from his voice.

"Of course we have, or you wouldn't have had an apartment to arrive to. They were serious about the vacancy over winter. If the owner couldn't move into a finished apartment, they had a quick sale. The first and second floors are completely sold." Her gaze moved to the bed. "I'd lived in a room the size of a closet for years. I tried sleeping in here one night and... I couldn't."

Markus released her hand and walked to the center of the airy master bedroom. If he weren't selfish, he'd ask if she were certain she still wanted to be his wife, his mate. An empty home made him doubt her initial decision. Circumstances beyond either of their control had led to a rushed union. Now he had to wonder if she harbored regret. If she wanted out. But he *was* selfish, and he couldn't fathom a future that no longer included her.

So.

One problem at a time.

Furniture, and her reluctance to turn their apartment into a home, was not the immediate issue. How they were going to handle their panicky guest and his problem came first. "My high marshal agreed to allow me to live in Sziveria, providing I accept critical assignments for a decade."

Shock slapped Bella's face. "A decade? How often can they call on you?"

Markus shrugged. "As often as needed, but the duties can't last longer than a month."

"What about winters?"

"I will try my hardest to be home for all the arctic-bound months."

"You didn't mention this in your letters," she whispered.

"I didn't get the specifics until two days before I left. And would the information have changed anything?"

"No, you know it wouldn't have."

She wrapped her arms around her waist and wandered to the floor-to-ceiling glass doors leading out to the sunroom. A few little plants sat in pots on shelves painted white. The sun broke through clouds. The slash of harsh light illuminated her gorgeous pale brown skin and the rich brown curls piled in a messy twist atop her head. He preferred the mass to be wild and untamed, framing her pretty face. In the unforgiving sunlight, he noted the ragged condition of her coat. Several seams were mended, and patches not quite close enough in color broke up the navy blue wool.

Frustration welled within him again. As his wife, Bella no longer had to live in poverty. He'd transferred funds for her to make purchases for the apartment and for anything she and her mother needed during the long winter months, they'd been apart. Markus knew if he checked the balance, the account would be untouched. One. Problem. At. A. Time.

"I won't go to Thanzia without you. Not when our time together is limited and I have no idea when I'll be called away," Markus said.

"My job—"

"Is one you no longer need to work," he bit out and knew the moment the words released it was the absolutely wrong thing to say. She hunched even further into herself and Markus ground his teeth.

Nothing about his returning to Sziveria was going according to plan. Instead of greeting his bride with a proper hug and kiss, he'd had to keep her from falling into oncoming traffic because his wolf had no self-control. A stranger had interrupted their intimacy. And now he'd attacked the one sense of pride she took in herself. Markus hated the way her superiors treated her. Hated that she'd been relegated to a basement position because guardians— the so-called protectors of Sziveria— were jealous of her undocumented talent. While he'd never made a secret of his disdain, he'd been careful to respect her decision to remain an employee of the Sziverian National Investigative Division.

"You *know* why I need my job," she said, her words low and laced with anger. "The doors open for all non-essential personnel to return to work on April first, and I plan to be at my desk. C.G. will have completed his catalog of evidence by then and I'll have a huge workload for long storage."

Markus clenched and released his fists. "Then I will tell Mr. Kavont he'll have to try to find someone else."

Bella slashed a hand through the air. "Don't be ridiculous. What he needs you for is important."

Markus closed the space between them and grasped her shoulders, turning her to face him. "Not as important as you. As us. I will not go without you. I'm not compromising on this."

"Hossman—"

"Will get his money," Markus ground out, wishing she'd have allowed him to handle the weasel of a moneylender months ago.

She jutted out her chin in defiance. "Yes, he will because I will be paying him from my earnings."

Markus ground his teeth. "The raimarks in the Sziverian account are yours, too."

"But the debt is not yours, Markus. I made that clear when I agreed to contract with you."

"Then I will pay you to be my assistant from this moment forward. The Thanzia job will have a rate, as will any other investigation or protection assignment I'm asked to perform. Until we have a family, you can travel with me," he said. When doubt pinched her face and she opened her mouth, he held up his hand. "Don't even think of telling me you aren't qualified. We've sent two serial killers to prison, and the last time I would have died if not for you."

Taking a chance she'd reject not only the idea but him, Markus closed the space between them and took her hand. Encouraged when she didn't pull away, he brought her fingers to his chest. "Will you do this? Will you give up your basement position in favor of becoming my assistant?"

THE WARMTH of his skin caressing hers and the sensation of his heart beating steadily against her palm were almost enough to distract her. Bella wanted to curl her fingers into the solid strength beneath her hand. She wanted to get lost in the taste of his lips and the intensity of his passion. Anything to distract from his question.

Guilt, however, wouldn't allow her to so much as take a step closer.

For a fraction of a second, relief poured into her when she realized Markus might have to leave again. If he weren't under the same roof as her, he couldn't regret their contracting. Bella had no doubt at some point, he'd resent the bonding she'd forced on him. Even if she'd done so to save his life, she'd still taken away any choice he had in the matter. Being bonded to her, a gen-common debt-riddled nobody, was going to become crystal clear one day. She'd rather the revelation arrive *before* she lost more of her heart to the beast master.

Now, he wanted her at his side no matter where life took him. For the year she'd known him, Markus had carried an incorrect view of her. One she still couldn't fathom. An entire nation could not be wrong where she was concerned.

But oh, the temptation to say yes. To be at his side, his equal, in everything. He did that to her.

Put hopes in her heart, made her believe in the version of herself he saw. Tenderness softened his beautiful golden eyes as he brushed his fingers along her jaw until he encountered a stray curl, which he tucked behind her ear.

"Come on, Bella. Agree. We can do this. Together," he whispered.

The thought of walking into the Sziverian National Intelligence Division and quitting the work she'd desperately needed and had been thankful to have, brought an ache to her chest. She took a deep breath and pulled her hand free. "What if jobs are once or twice a year? How will I make enough to pay my father's debt then?"

His hand shot toward the door and his eyes went wide. "Just stepped into the city."

Okay, so yes, word had spread rather quickly who'd been responsible for solving some unsolvable or even unknown cases. With Wolvenguard referring him now? Everyone would be knocking on their apartment door. The word of an arch guardian carried substantial weight. If things went well in Thanzia, Leander would return home praising Markus. The beast master would be turning jobs away. What, really, did she have to lose?

"All right, fine, but I'll have to resign before we leave. I'm not quitting by not showing up. If I ever need another job—"

"I agree, we'll go on our way back to the MagnaRail station." Markus bumped his knuckles under her chin until she looked at him. Then he kissed her. A slow, sensual melding of his lips to hers. "Thank you."

"Mmm," was all she managed, tipping forward when he pulled back.

He grasped her shoulders and steadied her teetering frame. Bella blinked and pressed a hand to the glass wall of their sunroom. He brushed his thumb across her lips, his gaze dark.

"So many delicious things I want this mouth to do," he rumbled.

A heady, captivating sensation zipped straight to her core. The tip of her tongue darted out to touch his thumb. He blinked and snatched his hand away.

"*Krahet'sna kovetka,* but you tempt me." He took a large step back. "Pack your bags, enough for two weeks with laundry."

And then he was gone, leaving the scent of rain drenched forest, leather, and man in his wake. Bella took a deep breath. She'd missed everything about him except for the way he disrupted her existence, turning her world into an upheaval she didn't know how to manage emotionally.

Below their apartment, Haven City moved through its routine. Living so close to Extilis Square meant a lot of visible traffic, the who's who of the city being seen on their way to the popular shopping destination. Bella watched for a few moments, light glinting off polished carriages and the glass windows of Ariots as they crawled by in heavy congestion. When she felt a bit more balanced, she left the near empty room for her own.

Low male voices rumbled from the dining area. Bella sped past, not wanting to get drawn into any conversation Markus may be having. The case wasn't hers, and she'd learned the hard way not to bring her opinion with matters involving Gen-Heirs. Not that Markus ever treated her as though her input never mattered, but rather the opposite. Leander may be among the elite guardians who felt his genetic inheritance set him apart, or rather above, someone like her. Best not to find out.

Lunah was lying on a rug in the middle of Bella's bedroom floor. The beautiful wolf raised her gray head, yawning her dark muzzle. Sharp teeth flashed in the lamplight. Bella's room didn't have a window. For years, where she slept hadn't had one, and after all the changes, she'd been drawn to the familiar. Bella patted Lunah's head on her way to the closet. A real closet of her very own. She'd been more than happy for *that* improvement. After pulling out a travel bag, she tossed it on the bed and then began packing.

"Your alpha wants me to go to another country with you," Bella sighed, throwing in a shirt and two pairs of flowy pants. She didn't know much about Thanzia other than it was an arid land near the coast with sandy soil and lush enough for cotton to thrive inland.

A faint painful sensation bloomed in her head and she touched her temples. The discomfort always developed when Lunah opened the bond, something only the wolf could manage. Bella still didn't fully understand the connection between them, only that the ability for her to establish one was rare since Bella's Ruthenian heritage was far removed. Closing her eyes for a second, she took a centering breath. The discomfort increased.

I missed you, my Bella, I missed you, Lunah whispered in her mind.

Bella sat on the bed. Lunah stepped between her legs and laid her muzzle on Bella's thigh. "I missed you too, pretty girl."

I hurt you, I hurt.

Bella patted between the wolf's ears, a smile working free through the ache. "You were very excited."

A long whine growled from Lunah's throat. *I will do better, I will.*

Bella scratched under the wolf's chin and around behind her ears. "We're both learning."

The rough, spongy texture of Lunah's tongue ghosted along Bella's forearm. *Do not want to be separated again, do not.*

Bella pulled Lunah's face close, touching her nose to the wolf's damp snout. "We won't, I promise. Not for a little while anyway."

A soft knock interrupted their conversation. Bella shook her head, still unable to believe she *could* have a conversation with a dog. And be understood! The headache faded into nothing as Lunah slipped from her mind. Bella gave Lunah one last pat and stood from the bed.

"It's open," she called, not having remembered closing the door.

The hinges squeaked a second before Markus filled the frame. He stuffed his hands into his pants pockets and regarded them. "Leander is going to pick up his bag. He was already packed and had a MagnaRail ticket purchased for a cabin. We'll have to add you."

Bella crossed the room to her dressing table and grabbed toiletries. She tossed them into the bag. "I'm almost finished."

Markus entered her room and glanced around. He looked from her narrow bed to the hand drawings covering her walls, to the well-worn dresser. Not much had changed from what he'd remember about her room in their tiny house in The Rows. Bella focused on finishing her packing rather than examining the frustration he'd likely have on his face.

"Dresser is new."

"It was my mother's," Bella said, opening a drawer and removing undergarments. "Her closet had drawers and shelves, so she no longer needed it."

"Bella," he whispered close enough to stir the hair on the back of her neck.

Gasping, she spun and found herself pinned to the dresser. His hands braced on the surface beside her hips, trapping her. The golden hue of his eyes was muted in the weak lamp light but not the intensity of his expression. He'd always moved with a disturbing silence.

"Do you want to be married to me?" he asked, voice still soft.

Bella's heart thumped hard. "What? Why... do you not..." She licked her suddenly dry lips. "Are you, I mean, have y—"

He kissed her. His tongue slid inside her mouth easily since she'd been mid-word. Bella groaned at the sensation of his lips over hers, his body pressing close and his tongue stroking a wicked path. She clutched at the front of his jacket, finding herself hating the garment for the second time in less than an hour. He lifted her to sit on top of the dresser and she didn't hesitate to part her legs to make room for his hips.

His arms banded around her, jerking her into the wall of his chest. Bella hugged his neck and pressed close. The heat of his touch sizzled along the bare skin of her back. Down to her hips, where he flexed his fingers and then ventured lower... until his palms cupped her rear, causing the waist of her pants to pull tight across her stomach. She wanted the same. To have him under hand. Only once had she experienced the pleasure of touching his skin, of seeing him. At the time, however, he'd been half dead, recovering from being almost fully dead.

Certainly wasn't the situation now, her husband was healthy in *every* aspect.

He hoisted her up and spun them around as she wrapped her legs around his hips. Two steps had them toppling onto her tiny bed. The frame creaked and groaned under their combined weight. Breathing heavily, Bella lifted her hips while yanking on his jacket. Buttons popped free and she almost wept.

Only Markus had ever brought her to desperate heights to know what happened beyond a kiss. For the last six months, she'd existed on her fantasies alone, and she *knew* they'd be laughable in comparison to the actual experience. He moved one hand from her rear to her hip, sliding under the waistband of her pants to tease the sensitive skin of her abdomen.

A rapid series of knocks reverberated through the apartment. Markus let loose a volley of Ruthenian, frustration clear in his voice. Bella growled her own disappointment. He dropped his forehead to hers.

"Yes, I want to be married to you. Soon, mated to you properly. I just wasn't sure how you felt because this is our home, and... you only live in this room," he said quietly in the intimate space between them. "I wasn't sure."

That he, a strong, confident man, could be brought to any sort of doubt left her blinking. She brushed her fingers along his bearded jaw, taking in the strong angles of his face. "I missed you so much."

He pressed a tender kiss to her lips. "I missed you, too."

"I told you why I didn't furnish the apartment. I wasn't lying. I wanted us to build our home together."

Pound, pound, pound. The front door shook in the frame. He hefted himself onto his arms and glanced over his shoulder. Bella slid her hands along his jaw and brought his gaze back to her.

"Markus," she said, tracing his cheek to his nose and down to his lips. She needed to reassure him before they were interrupted. Again. "I haven't stopped wanting to be married to you."

He brushed his mouth to hers. "The day we return."

"Straight to the first furniture market in Extilis Square," she said, laughing. She lowered her arms and caressed his shoulders to his biceps, where she squeezed and then released him. "Are you packed?"

A muffled voice shouting echoed with another hard knock. Groaning, Markus rose and straightened his coat. "I have my bag from the ship. I'll have to do laundry at some point, but if we're taking a passenger ship to Thanzia, I can wash onboard."

Bella scooted to the edge of the bed and pulled her bag closer to double-check what she'd packed. "I'll grab it if you'll get the front door."

"I'm shocked they haven't given up yet."

Grumbling, Markus sauntered from the room. Bella appreciated the view of his fit form striding away. She closed the latches on her bag and slid the strap onto her shoulder. Before leaving her room, she grabbed a few books to put into her messenger bag. She placed the books and her duffel on the dining table. Markus blocked the doorway, one hand on the door, the other on the frame. He nodded as a man spoke on the other side. Bella lifted her brows, wondering if another emergency had landed on their doorstep.

She found Markus's bag slung on top of the chests. Before she could pick it up, Markus was there hefting the strap onto his shoulder.

"Are you ready?" he asked.

"Yes."

"Good, if you want to make the stop at the SNID, we have to leave now. Leander sent a carriage to pick us up, but the driver has another stop scheduled in an hour."

Ah. Hence the frantic knocking. Bella collected her travel and messenger bag. On a last thought, she grabbed a slip of paper and wrote her mother a quick note. Madeleine would not be happy she hadn't been able to say hello to Markus or goodbye to her daughter, but she'd understand. Bella smiled. Her mother always understood. Bella would be sure to find her a special gift in Thanzia.

After Lunah followed them out, Markus locked the door. The driver was already downstairs. Markus sighed as he held the door to the stairs open for Bella and Lunah.

"What?" she asked, squeezing past with her belongings.

"I was ready to be home."

She caressed her hand along his jaw. "I was ready for that, too."

And much more. But she didn't have the courage to voice her disappointment.

He grasped her fingers and kissed them. The wicked gleam in his eyes told her spoken desires were unnecessary. "Soon."

Voices echoed under the soaring glass roof of the MagnaRail station, joining with the rush of wind, the hiss and squeal of steel-on-steel, and the physical, bass hum of massive engines engaging. Bella wanted to cover her ears, but figured the action would be both childish *and* peg her as an easy mark for the pick-pockets. Not that she had much to pilfer. No fancy jewelry or extra raimarks. The only adornments she wore were the leather bracer Markus had placed on her left wrist as a pseudo-promise band that she hadn't been able to remove even after a silver wedding band had arrived for her.

Her husband was a different situation. Multiple silver rings flashed on his large hands, and she knew underneath his jacket sleeves, he'd have leather bracers that matched hers. However, the wolf loping at his side helped discourage anyone who thought to brave getting close to her towering husband.

"Over there!" Markus shouted over the cacophony of sound, pointing.

Bella rose on her tiptoes to see over the crowd. At five-foot-ten-inches, she had an advantage. She followed his arm and spotted Leander pacing in front of an almost empty queue. A few stragglers rushed through the rope maze. Markus bumped and shoved his way through the thick crowd of the overflowing line to get on the next train. Bella grabbed hold of his jacket to keep from getting jostled and he reached behind, taking her hand. Finally, they broke through the congestion and into the vacant line. His grip tightened as they wove around the barrier ropes.

"Oh, thank goodness," Leander said, bending over and propping his hands on his thighs, "I was sure you'd miss the train." He stood and shoved an envelope at Markus. "Here are your boarding passes."

"One for Bella, too?" Markus asked, accepting the tickets.

"Yes." Leander walked sideways, waving at the train. "Now, please, let's get on before they leave without us."

Since they were in a cabin, they kept their personal belongings. Bella had been on a Magna-Rail train once in her life when they'd taken a family vacation to Sunwater Cove, a quaint seaside town on the southern coast. A long train ride in coach and an even longer carriage ride along bumpy, sand-filled roads. The week spent at the beach had been worth the journey. They entered the seventh car, and Markus had to turn sideways to fit down the narrow corridor leading to all the private cabins. Leander led the way, stopping to open the accordion-style door. He disappeared inside and Bella followed, pausing at the entry.

"Um…" She blinked at the tiny room.

"Go on in, people are waiting and they can't get past me," Markus said, gently urging her into the tight enclosure.

Bella exhaled her doubt and shifted inside. Lunah followed, taking up all the floor space from her muzzle to her fluffy slate-gray tail. Markus squished in behind her, curling her tail along her side before closing them in.

"Your bags can—oh!" Leander toppled onto the short bench seat across from the one Bella's thighs were pressed against. His curls bounced atop his head and he blinked behind his frames as he pushed them up his nose. "Oh my. We're a bit, uh, cramped, aren't we?"

"Little bit," Bella said, squeezing into the corner. Markus wrestled with shoving their belongings into the overhead bin.

Leander pulled his feet onto the bench, wrapping his arms around his legs. "I hadn't realized…" Another push of the glasses. "That the, um, wolf, would be joining us."

"I'm a beast master, Mr. Kavont," Markus stated mid shove. "No wolf, no me."

Leander cleared his throat. "Yes, of course. She doesn't, uh, she doesn't bite, does she?"

Markus's smile was anything but reassuring. "Only when I tell her to."

Leander turned into a tighter ball. "Right."

Bella pressed her lips together to keep from laughing. She sat, adjusting her messenger bag to fit in the space between her and the wall. A window took up most of the wall, a thick, emerald-green curtain pulled back and secured by hooks. A table was folded and locked underneath. With Lunah in the car with them, they wouldn't be using the surface. Markus sat next to her, taking her hand and placing it on his leg. The action was surprisingly intimate, like he couldn't go a moment without touching her. His strong thigh flexed under her palm.

Leander shifted on the padded green velvet bench until he could fit his entire body comfortably on the seat. Lunah chuffed as if the academic man amused her. The cabin rocked gently before a faint hiss sounded, and the rail car jerked upward. An impression of floating had Bella gripping Markus's leg, the weightless sensation causing her stomach to flop. And then they were moving, a gradual rise in speed until the city was nothing more than a blur gliding past the window.

Leander didn't remove his gaze from Lunah, who settled to lay her head on her front paws. Her tail swished a slow arc, brushing the wood paneling. She yawned through a low growly whine, her sharp teeth flashing before she licked her muzzle and settled. Leander's nose twitched, causing his pencil-thin mustache to jump around. Bella covered her mouth to hide her urge to laugh again.

"Why don't you tell us about Thanzia, Mr. Kavont," Markus said, lacing his fingers through hers. "Are there any customs we should know about to keep from offending anyone?"

Leander straightened and dove into a long

and extended discussion about Thanzia from an anthropologist's perspective, giving them detailed histories, traditions, and social practices. The fear disappeared from his body language, replaced with a passion for the culture. Markus slid Bella a sideways glance and winked.

The enthusiastic explanation would have continued until they fell into a stupor if not for a rapid knock on the thin accordion door. The conductor announced himself before sliding open the partition. While the education in cultural norms, observed rituals and theorized history was all very fascinating, Leander seemed to forget his audience wasn't among the academics he normally conversed with. Bella didn't understand half the lingo he tossed around. Or why she needed to know Thanzian children didn't bury their teeth with seeds to grow a plant like Sziverians did, but rather they were kept to eventually be buried with their owner, a complete circle being represented. Interesting, but doubtful a necessity for them to help investigate a missing archeologist.

Markus handed over their tickets while Leander rummaged around in his jacket for the envelope containing his. The conductor signed his name on the necessary line, informing them during the process that the dining car was open for meals, snacks, and drinks. Leander handed over his ticket. The conductor finished authorizing their passage and left with a tip of his hat.

Markus stood, stretched, brushing the ceiling in the process. "I'm going to get something to eat, anyone else?"

"Yes, I would very much like something to eat, but ah," Leander waved a hand at Lunah, "I don't know how to get up from my seat here. Perhaps you could move her to the corridor?"

Bella patted the cushion next to her. "Come up here, my girlie."

Lunah climbed her furry form onto the bench. Her tail thumped a happy rhythm against the wooden back. The wolf shoved her muzzle under Bella's arms. Laughing, Bella played with Lunah's ears, flopping them back and forth.

Leander inched off his seat and then dove for the door, colliding with Markus on his way out. Markus kept the man from falling on his face, steadying him in the hall. When Markus was sure Leander wouldn't topple over, he patted the man's thin shoulder and gave Bella a thumbs up before closing her and his wolf inside.

Lunah licked under Bella's jaw before settling her paws on Bella's lap and pressing her nose to the window. She chuffed softly at the scenery speeding by. Bella brushed her fingers through the thick fur of Lunah's back, letting the soft texture soothe her nerves.

The men returned with drinks and snacks. Markus scooted Lunah off the seat. She moved to the floor but continued watching out the window. The ground gave way to a canyon with a river below. Sun sparkled off the water, turning the water into liquid gold. A flock of birds flew under the bridge and Lunah woofed softly, leaving a vapor bloom across the glass.

Leander sat as far as possible from Lunah on the bench. He placed the food on his lap and the drink in a holder he'd pulled down from the center of the seat. Markus handed Bella a wax paper bag and a jar with a lid and glass straw. She took a sip. Bubbly sweetness exploded across her tongue. Surprised, she pulled the drink back. Strawberries floated in rich, effervescent liquid.

Markus took a pull from his glass. "Strawberry soda with cream."

Bella took another drink. "Mmm, thank you, it's delicious."

The bag contained a pressed ham and cheese sandwich. Lunah twisted around and lay at Markus's feet the moment he opened his bag. Her body contorted into the narrow space, her tail swished into the curtains across from Bella. The duo did their eating routine. Markus took a bite of his food and then offered Lunah hers. Leander watched with big eyes behind his lenses. The wolf didn't snatch the bite from her alpha's hand, she gently nibbled his fingers until he released. Only then did she gobble the morsel as though she hadn't eaten in days. Licking her muzzle, her golden eyes stared at him with rapt attention, and the process repeated.

"I have never witnessed the bond in action before," Leander whispered, clearly worried he'd break said bond if he spoke too loudly.

Bella pulled her sandwich halves apart. Gooey, melted cheese dangled from the pieces, and she lifted it up high to capture as much in her mouth as she could. The savory flavor paired well with her sweet drink. "Their connection isn't weak. Nothing you do or say will interrupt them."

"So I can...." He lifted the bag on his lap and shook it.

Bella wiggled her sandwich half and then took a huge bite, leaned in close to Lunah, and made *num-num* sounds. Lunah licked Bella's nose and then went back to focusing on Markus, the food in Bella's hand ignored.

Leander exhaled. "All right, then. Very good."

After they finished eating, Markus took Lunah for a walk, and Leander settled lengthwise on his side and disappeared into his work. Books were soon piled next to his thighs and papers littered the seat. Bella watched the scenery pass by, marveling at the geographical changes. From dark forests to sprawling fields of emerging flowers to rocky outcroppings so tall, they formed their own sort of canyons. Markus and Lunah returned, settling.

The time passed in amicable silence. Light shifted from blazing day to subdued evening into the night and Bella wondered how they'd all sleep in such a tiny car. They were scheduled to arrive around nine the following morning. Turned out she had nothing much to worry about. Leander fell asleep sitting up, a book open on his lap. Bella drifted off, and when she awoke, she was lying on the bench, her head on Markus's lap. Somehow, he'd moved both himself and her without waking her. A thin, knit blanket was draped over her. His fingers combed through her hair, from her temple to her shoulder.

Bella rolled onto her back and brushed her fingers along the column of his neck. He shifted until their eyes met in the darkness. "You can't be comfortable," she whispered.

He grasped her hand and kissed her knuckles. "Go back to sleep, I'm exactly where I want to be."

And with those words, the fierceness of her love for this man tightened like a fist in her chest. She wanted to wrap around him, experience the passion only he could call forth within her, taste—

"Enough," he growled. "I know, and we're stuck in a box of a room with company."

"The bond?" she asked quietly in wonder. "You can…"

He leaned down, cupped her head, and pressed a gentle kiss to her lips. "Only the strongest of emotions."

Leander muttered. A reminder they weren't alone. Papers crinkled and a book tumbled to the floor. Lunah grumbled but remained lying, paws curled into her chest, lower legs flopped wide. Sighing, Markus straightened, dropping his hand. Bella shoved her desire down deep and sat up enough to peer out the window. Shadowy trees sped past, the night an inky black void beyond.

"Do you know where we are?" she asked.

"I think we passed the Ironwood Correctional Facility turn off about a half hour ago."

Bella raised her brows and tried to visualize the rail line. "We're close. They made great time."

"They didn't stop at two stations, no passengers to pick up. I think we have another two hours or so."

Bella laid back down but doubted she'd get any more sleep. In a few hours, she'd board a ship for the very first time. She'd be leaving her country. The reality of setting foot on soil, not of her homeland, brought a wave of apprehension. Why did she let Markus talk her into going? She should be keeping her head low in her basement position. Paying back her father's debt in the familiar method she knew. She wasn't an adventurer. Everything was about to change in so many ways. The SNID had accepted her resignation with an ease that physically hurt. Of course, they hadn't needed her nearly as much as she'd needed them. The reminder had stung.

Markus returned to the soothing caress of her hair. Bella closed her eyes and forced her mind to empty. The course was set for her future now. Literally. Underneath her cheek, Markus's thigh flexed, a subtle reminder no matter how anxious her world became, she wouldn't be handling it alone. And hopefully, in the coming weeks, when her ineptitude became wholly apparent, he wouldn't regret asking her to join in the investigation. And maybe Bella would surprise herself. She wanted to. She wanted to be what he seemed to see and not the mediocre person everyone else accepted— or rather demanded— she be.

FOUR

THE SHIP ROSE AND FELL UNDER YET ANOTHER ROLLING wave. The ice flows may have melted enough to traverse the Black Ocean south of the Sovereign Channel, but the conditions were still rough. Markus held Bella's hair back as she heaved into a porcelain water bowl. She wouldn't have made it across the hall to the community bathroom. Markus had learned over the last week when she'd be able to make the short trip or when he needed to make a mad dash for the bowl in their room. This bout of seasickness had been a bowl grab. The ocean had not been kind to his bride.

Bella collapsed back onto the narrow bunk. Their room was a modest berth with three narrow bunks that folded up into the wall to create more floor space or somewhere to sit. Across from the bunks, a single storage locker had all their belongings crammed inside. A small corner table had magnets to keep the bowl and pitcher in place. Leander had taken the very top bunk, Markus in the middle and Bella on the bottom. Lunah slept either curled up with Markus or

Bella or beneath Bella. A small porthole revealed the endless ocean with its white-capped waves. The constant motion, both inside and out, had led to Markus being on sick duty.

Markus left to clean the bowl with Lunah to stretch her legs. He took a detour after washing the basin to grab some baked crackers from the dining room. The elegant space was so different from their room, but they'd been given what was left available for multiple travelers. Being the first ship to sail south for the year meant a full register. The lack of privacy for the three, combined with Bella's intolerance to oceanic travel, had made the journey miserable.

Weaving through the linen-draped tables and the soft chime of the crystal chandeliers swaying, Markus found the complementary snack table at the back of the room. Baskets of wrapped cookies, crackers, dried meat, and glass jars of fresh water were arranged in neat rows. Little holes in the top allowed for glass straws to keep anything from spilling. Markus grabbed a wicker basket for carrying the items and loaded up enough water and snacks for them all, including some extra jerky for Lunah.

Everything was as he'd left it in their room. He placed the clean bowl on the table, the magnet making a loud *thunk*. He tossed the water and a handful of snacks up to Leander, who muttered his appreciation. One jar in hand, along with a pack of crackers, he crawled into Bella's tight space and pulled her into his arms. Lunah settled on the floor with her jerky treat.

"Drink something, *krahet'sna*, or you'll be

sicker." He brought the glass straw to her dry lips.

She took a tentative sip, grimaced, and pushed his hand away. "I can't."

"You can. I have some crackers, too." He wrapped her hand around the jar. "You know the process."

She groaned and tried to turn away, but he'd been expecting her resistance and kept her in place, placing a nibble of cracker in her mouth. A weightless sensation preceded a heavy shudder through the berth, followed by a lurching rise. Markus glanced out the window and noted the massive wave rolling past.

"That was a big one."

Bella moaned and twisted to press her face into his chest. "I'm going to be sick again."

TRAVEL-WEARY AND EXHAUSTED, Markus guided Bella down the ramp onto dry land. Finally. Around them, Zarsina Port was a hive of early morning activity. Passenger ships from across the Atlantic, along with the Black Ocean, crowded the docks. Outbound merchant ships had crated wares stacked high enough to block the sun, the crews working in impressive teams to load.

Bella staggered and Markus caught her arm to keep her upright. Leander grabbed Markus's other arm to steady himself. While he hadn't been sick like Bella, the poor academic hadn't been able to sleep with the constant movement. Dark bags drooped under his eyes, and fatigue grayed his skin.

"Do you want to stay in Zarsina, or get to Lagosin City to rest?" Markus asked, guiding his little group to where carriages for hire were lined up waiting for patrons. Cool, salt-tinged wind gusted, whipping his jacket and braid around his back, and made Lunah's fur dance.

"Lagosin City," Bella answered. "I want to get to where we're going and sleep for a day straight."

Leander grunted his agreement. The route through the crowd was easy, thanks to Lunah, who led the way. Markus opened the door to the carriage and helped everyone inside with their belongings. He hopped in after Leander gave the driver directions in Thanzian. Lunah jumped inside last, taking her place on the floor while Markus closed them in. Bella laid her head back against the dark stained wood, eyes closed.

Markus took her hand, his chest tight from her discomfort. "We're almost done."

"It's around a three-hour ride to Lagosin City," Leander said, pushing his glasses up as the carriage jerked into motion. "Thanzian roads are well designed, brick or stone the entire way."

In Sziveria, paved roads were only in high population areas. Ruthenia was a mix, keeping main travel roads between cities paved, while more obscure routes tended to remain dirt. Markus always appreciated countries that placed pride in their roads.

Sandy flats with tuffs of wheatgrass and foothills in the distance made the land unfolding around them feel barren and dry. Huts with thatched roofs and more impressive concrete buildings with wrought iron balconies dotted the landscape. Little open-air shops providing the locals with necessities were opening for the day, setting their products on tables, or hanging them along the edges to catch shoppers' attention. A dusty haze, haloed by the early sun, gave Zarsina a magical quality.

Markus wanted to point out the sights to Bella, but she hadn't opened her eyes, so he settled back and watched the beauty of Thanzia alone. Disappointment once again settled like a stone in his belly. None of the misfortune to befall them since their reunion was either of their faults. And yet, he couldn't help but be unnerved by all the elements that conspired to keep them apart. He sat inches from her, but she might as well have remained in Sziveria. Lunah shifted to sit between his knees. She rested her head on his thigh.

All will be well, all will be, she said gently, nudging his forearm with her nose.

I know. Markus slid his hands into her fur and leaned his head back.

Then he remembered the flutter of desire that had skated across his nerves on the train when in the darkness, they had the illusion of finally being alone. They may not have been given the privacy they'd earned with their months apart, but her emotions couldn't lie to him. Any frustration he had didn't belong directed at his relationship. Markus wrapped an arm around Bella's shoulders and pulled her into his side. She sighed and melted against his frame. No resistance. He kissed the top of her head and caressed up and down her back.

"I wish I had the energy to give you a proper tour as we travel," Leander muttered, his head rolling along the wood. His curls were crazier than usual. Markus wasn't sure if the man had bothered to comb them after the first sleepless night. "There is such rich history in this land."

"I think every land has a rich history," Markus said.

"Ah, yes, of course. However, the drier climate, combined with being more centrally located on the planet, means the arctic winds don't bring the cold like they do for those of us north of the Black Ocean. They do experience seasonal change, but nothing drastic such as twelve feet of snow for a month or longer. Their history has been able to be preserved in a spectacular fashion. Most of the buildings you see, even the huts, are well over a hundred years old."

The buildings became more sporadic until only gently rolling land butted up against foothills dotted with shrubbery. Grains of sand chased each other in drifts across the ground, the sight familiar to winter back home. Bella's weight soon slumped into a boneless mass against his body. He hugged her close, holding her through the sway and bumps of the journey. With his mate in his arms and his wolf on his lap, Markus had his whole world.

Three hours later, they pulled up to a three-story building. Plaster painted in vivid green trimmed with orange coated the hotel and made it stand out from the surrounding buildings, which were boring, unadorned sandstone. A flower-lined walkway led to a lavender door. Blooming vines spilled from planters hung at every window. Markus opened the carriage door and Lunah bounded out, bouncing along the cement path, sniffing every few feet to the door.

Leander stumbled out and accepted his bag from the driver while handing him a handful of coins without counting. The driver sputtered and tried to catch Leander's attention, but the academic had already wandered out of reach. Markus shook his head, hoping the exhausted man hadn't just handed over all his funds. When Bella didn't so much as twitch from her half-upright position, Markus gathered her in his arms and carried her from the carriage. The driver handled their bags without being asked, an obvious bonus to having been overpaid.

Inside, the establishment was as vibrant as the outside. Woven rugs in bright, geometric patterns littered the floor and hung from the walls, which were various shades of orange and yellow. Furniture painted white invited guests to sit around mosaic-tiled tables of various heights and sizes. A tall, dark-skinned man straightened from watering one of the many plants hanging from the ceiling. He smiled in greeting and waved to a check-in counter.

"How can I help with you?" he asked, his words heavily accented and spoken in Atlantic, the language common for Sziveria, Westica, Monaco Sands, and Miami Island. Though not quite proper, which made Markus smile.

"Do we have a reservation?" Markus asked Leander.

"Ah, yes." Leander patted his pockets and then set his stuffed messenger bag on the counter. He dug around inside and pulled out a crumbled yellow paper. After smoothing the edges, he slid the page to the innkeeper. "Here we are."

The innkeeper picked up the paper and grinned, showing it to them. "Most good!" He pressed a hand to his chest. "I thankful."

Leander mimicked the motion. "You're welcome."

"Welcome, yes!" The man grinned again, his smile bright against his chocolate skin. "I welcome the," he turned the paper and looked it over again, "Sziveria historical research team to my space."

Keys jingled and two sets were placed on the counter attached to orange tiles with blue painted numbers. The innkeeper touched his chest again. "I A'ki kwan Mah'ihumashi."

Leander made the proper introductions for their group to A'ki while Markus crouched low enough to wiggle a finger free and pick up the key to their room. Markus wondered if he'd ever tire of hearing his family name attached to Bella. Pride and a sense of possessiveness had him tightening his arms around her.

"I do not mean to be rude, but my mate needs her rest," he said after Leander finished speaking.

"Please, up this way." A'ki motioned to the polished stairs off to the right of the counter and took the lead. A long sash of maroon, sage green, and slate blue swayed from his left hip in individual lengths. "I fix two meals, morning and night. Day, I suggest city meals. Taste Thanzia, find new things."

Upstairs was open and airy. Long windows at each end of the corridor combined with cream walls and ash wood floors bounced light. Painted tiles depicting local wildlife hung between each closed door. Cobalt blue tiles edging the walls added an additional pop of color. A'ki fussed with each pedestaled fern he passed, fluffing the draping leaves or checking the soil. He stopped before a door on the left and motioned.

"One room." He indicated to the next door. "The other." He bowed. "I bring up bags. Please rest."

Leander pressed his hand to his chest. "We thank you, A'ki."

"Excellent service," Markus said after the innkeeper retreated.

"Lagosin City is a wonderful place. I always stay at this establishment when I come here." Leander paused at his door, looking around the corridor. "It's clean, beautiful, comfortable, and he makes fantastic meals. All things you want when you aren't home."

Markus shifted Bella in his arms and squatted low enough to slide the key into the lock. "I don't know if we'll be down for the meal."

"It's fine," Leander said, unlocking his own door. "A'ki will leave a tray outside the door for you."

"Until tomorrow, then." Markus pushed the

door open and went in first, using his foot to close then in after Lunah.

The wolf explored the spacious room. A long corridor led to a sitting area. A half wall separated the bedroom. A door directly to his left showed a pristine bathroom done in white and cobalt tile with a sunken shower stall, toilet, and square sink set into a modest counter space. Low, vivid yellow couches meant for lounging sat across from each other, a colorful blue rug making the hue all the brighter. Shelves set into the wall offered a vibrant array of local pottery work, from bowls to little figurines. Two wide windows offered light and a view.

Markus carried Bella to the bed and sat, adjusting her in his arms to brush his fingers across her face. "Bella, *mie krahet'sna*, wake up. We're in our room."

She stirred, her beautiful eyes blinking open. "Hmm?"

"I thought you'd want to at least shower before getting into the bed," he whispered, helping her sit. Once she was somewhat stable, he moved to the floor to help her remove her shoes.

She yawned and swayed, her eyes fluttering closed. "Mmm, a shower would be nice."

"You'll have to stay awake long enough to take one."

"Awake, yes," she mumbled.

Lunah padded into the room and gave a sharp yip. Bella jerked, her eyes going wide.

"What?" she said.

Markus chuckled, tossing her shoes out of the

way. He tugged on the bottom of her shirt. "Lift your arms."

Pink blossomed across her cheeks. "Oh, um, I can do that."

Markus braced his hands on the soft mattress on either side of her, his mouth brushing her ear. "I'll see it all soon, why not now?"

She fisted both her hands into the tunic. "Because."

Markus smiled and stepped away, motioning toward the bathroom. Her shyness was cute and, hopefully, soon, something she'd rarely feel in his presence again. But he'd not pressure her. "Bathroom is over there."

She stood, wobbled, held out a hand, and nodded once steady. Lunah pushed her muzzle under Bella's hand and sat when petted. "Where are our bags?"

"Probably out in the hall. I'll set yours in the bathroom for you."

She blinked, dropping her hand to her side. "Did I really sleep through check-in and...." She glanced at the window. "Wow, being carried upstairs, apparently."

"You did."

She scrubbed a hand down her face. "All right, let me get a shower."

"We aren't expected anywhere after this. Get cleaned up, and we'll go to bed early."

A long sigh left her. "Yes, that's perfect."

Markus collected their belongings while she disappeared into the bathroom. He briefly stood outside the bathroom door, listening to the water hit the tile. Picturing her lithe, naked body gleaming under the spray while soap bubbles raced down her pale brown skin had him pressing his forehead to the wood. Soon, he could join her, and he imagined her welcoming smile. Would she be seductive, maybe a little timid, or perhaps bold? He couldn't wait to learn all her intimate secrets.

They may be able to claim having known each other for a year, but he knew so little about her in person. He was impatient to discover what she liked, from food to colors to how she wanted to be touched by him. The waiting was making him edgy, and the lack of privacy since being re-united didn't help. Finally, he had her alone, but she was exhausted. He'd be content to keep holding her, relishing in the strength and heat of her body pressed to his.

Opening the door, he slipped her bag inside and resisted the urge to sneak a peek. There'd been no curtain or wall. But why cause himself more pain than he was already in? He shut the door on temptation and went to get the room ready. Shutters closed to block light, and curtains stopped any bleeding from the edges. Relocating a rug to provide a comfortable space for Lunah. A bedside lamp produced enough illumination for him to pull the blankets down and toss excess pillows.

After stripping to boxers, he climbed between the cool cotton sheets. The door to the bathroom creaked open.

"Markus?" Bella called.

"In bed." He patted the mattress. "Come on."

"It's so dark." She shuffled to the bedroom, her form heavily shadowed. "Where's Lunah?"

"Curled up over here, on my side of the bed."

The mattress depressed as she sat. She wore a thin slip of a nightgown that left nothing to the imagination. Markus took a slow visual journey down her body. The cream satin made the rich tone of her skin glow, molded to her small breasts, showed the perfect outline of her nipples, draped over her flat stomach, hugged the soft curve of her hips, and bunched at her sleek thighs. Markus choked back a groan. Rolling over, he doused the light before he scared her with the tent action he had the blankets doing.

While sleeping together wasn't exactly new for them, he'd occupied her bunk plenty during the voyage, they hadn't been alone. The way she hesitated to slip between the blankets betrayed her nerves. Markus brushed his hand across her hip. Her breath hitched, and she jumped.

"We're just going to sleep," he whispered, curling his fingers into her side and pulling her down. He kissed her temple when she settled onto the pillow. Her curls caught in his beard and tickled his nose. "Just sleep."

She grasped the edge of the sheet as he pulled it over her chest. "But you want more."

He propped himself up on his elbow, even though he couldn't see much in the darkness. "*Dak.*" Tenderly, he explored her face, tracing the delicate angles by touch. "I want you so much I ache." He grazed another kiss across her temple. "When I take you, you won't be exhausted or recovering. And you certainly won't be nervous or unsure. Now sleep."

Her fingers fluttered along his jaw, smoothing into his beard and up to his hair. "I'm not unsure about anything where you're concerned."

Grasping her hand, he kissed her fingers and smiled. "Nervous, however."

She pulled her hand free and slipped his braid over his shoulder. "A little."

"Sleep, or I'll be too tempted to show you there's nothing to be worried about."

A faint tug on his braid brought his mouth to hers. She kissed him, soft and sweet. "You're making it hard to think about sleep."

"Hard, *dak*, that is the word," he rumbled.

She chuckled and tugged on his braid again. A shudder raced along her entire body. Markus smoothed his fingers down to her throat, where her pulse beat a frantic rhythm. He leaned closer and licked along the racing flutter. Her breath hitched.

"Relax and rest," he whispered. He laid down and wrapped his arm around her waist. Nothing more. Not today.

The minutes crept by until she stopped trembling, and her breathing eased. Markus inhaled her sugary vanilla and succulent berry scent in deep. His fingers curled into the lushness of her belly, soft and warm beneath his palm. A few inches south, he'd discover something equally warm and soft. Oh, the desperation with which he *wanted*. Markus squeezed his eyes closed.

Soon.

CHAPTER

FIVE

A HAZY SENSATION ACROSS HER BARE STOMACH EASED Bella from sleep. Something tugged at her mind, a reason why she should be concerned about her belly being exposed. A masculine rumble had her eyes fluttering open. Stretching, Bella yawned and noted the cool air on her skin. She glanced down and remembered she'd dressed for bed like normal, in a nightgown with nothing on underneath. A habit she hadn't realized might matter until she sat on the bed next to her husband. Then she'd almost bolted back to the bathroom to dig around in her bag and find a clean pair of panties. But he'd made no moves or had any expectations, sincere in his desire for her to rest, and she'd forgotten about her being naked beneath the satin.

The darkness kept her nudity hidden, but if his hand moved down... Bella sucked in a breath. Instead of the near paralyzing nervousness of yesterday, an intriguing desire to discover how his touch would feel had Bella's hips shifting under his lazy questing. His mostly asleep state, combined with the dimness of their room, emboldened her curiosity.

Bella knew how her fingers felt between her legs. She wanted to know if Markus could do better. She'd imagined, for months, that he could. Aside from her modesty, nothing stood between them now. According to him, he'd be with her forever. A prerequisite of hers that she knew had been lofty and perhaps a little naïve to hope for, and yet she'd found it in the man lying at her side. She had no reason to doubt him.

Anticipation thrummed at her core, the heady ache making her bite her lip. She grasped his wrist and guided his hand to the apex of her thighs, lifting her hips in expectation of his first touch. The tips of his fingers skimmed her clit, pressed, and slid to her opening. One finger eased into her and then back out. Pleasure spiked through her, and a gasp caught in her throat. Slick with her desire, his touch glided over her sensitive flesh, fluttering, teasing, bringing her to the brink. And suddenly, his touch wasn't enough.

"Markus," she moaned.

He shifted, his mouth touched to her shoulder, her collarbone, and up to her throat. His fingers slipped into her again, and Bella arched to take him deeper. He groaned, his tongue tracing along the cord of her neck. Out, slipped over her swollen clit, and back in, he repeated the maddening motions until she couldn't hold back a cry. Pressure built until she thought she'd scream from the need. She spread her legs wider to try to feel more and take him deeper as he played and teased.

Ruthenian tumbled from his mouth in hoarse gasps, and he moved closer until the length of his erection pressed into her hip. Bella grasped his bicep and held tight, wanting all of him and squirming in an effort to make her desires a reality. He took the hint, sliding his large frame over her. A few awkward but quick movements had them both naked, and Bella marveled at her lack of modesty in the heat of their moment. Bella tried to reach for him, curious about his body, which she'd tried her hardest to ignore the single time she'd had access.

Markus caught her hand and squeezed. "*Vye.* I won't make it even a second if you touch me, *krahet'sna.* I want you too much."

The words fueled her excitement and she pulled her knees up to his flanks. "Next time."

He groaned. "Oh *halrogva,* next time... I'm about to embarrass myself."

His hand shifted between their bodies, and she moaned in expectation as he positioned himself at her entrance. "Markus... please..."

Sweat dampened his skin, and Bella sucked in a breath when the head of his erection pressed into her. Finally, *finally*, she was going to experience passion.

Bang, bang, bang!

They both froze.

Bang, bang! "Ralstons? Are you in there? Are you both okay?" Another round of heavy knocks rattled their hotel room door. "Ralstons! Anyone? Hello?"

The doorknob jangled. Mumbled voices sounded. Bella squealed and shoved at Markus, though she didn't need to. He was in the process of leaping away. She scrambled for her nightgown. A muttered curse sounded in the dark seconds before the mattress vibrated.

"Do not open the door!" Markus bellowed, his accent thick.

Claws scrambled on the wood floor. Lunah growled and then barked. The voices quieted, and then a softer knock sounded.

"Are both the Ralstons well?" a new voice asked.

"We are fine. We'll be out in a moment," Markus said, his words clipped.

Fabric rustled and hinges squeaked. Bright light exploded into the room. Bella shielded her eyes, blinking.

"Damn," Markus muttered. "It must be almost lunchtime."

"What? You're kidding. We slept that long?" she asked, scrambling from the bed.

"I would have preferred all day in bed."

The heat in his voice made her look his way. Regret tightened his mouth and his gaze lingered on her body. Bella smoothed a hand down her stomach to ease the flutters inside. "Me too."

"I would come over there and kiss you good morning, but—"

She couldn't help chuckling. "We'd never stop at a kiss. I know."

"A good problem to have, I suppose."

Bella shook her head. "Not when we can't seem to catch a moment alone."

"At least we have our privacy when we return."

Unlike the rest of the time they'd traveled. "We should see if they have a way for us to ensure we won't be disturbed."

He paused in pulling a shirt from his bag. The muscles of his stomach flexed and the light gleamed off the dark hairs sprinkled over his chest. Bella wanted to explore every sensual inch of him.

"When we return, I will make sure no one bothers us. Not unless the building is on fire, and even that might be an exception," he rumbled, yanking a dark green shirt free.

Bella laughed. "Some things are worth potentially dying for, hmm?"

His gaze turned serious. "Right now, Mr. Kavont is lucky I won't strangle him. He has come between me and my mate, and nothing comes between us."

Sliding his arms into the shirt, he went to leave the bedroom area, and Bella gasped, rushing to close the distance between them. In the hard light streaming in through the open window, the detailed tattoo taking up his entire back seemed to glow. A frame of vines and roses morphed into a stunning wolf, who stared out at her with brilliant golden eyes, the only color in the entire work of art. Below the wolf, words in Ruthenian were scrawled in a masculine script.

Bella grasped the back of his arm and made him stop moving. Slowly, she slid his braid over his shoulder and traced the thicker lines of the tattoo. "This is unbelievable. I can't believe I didn't notice before."

"You'd only had one opportunity, and you wouldn't exactly look," he said.

She followed a curving vine to a full bloom near the center of his back. The indent created by his spine added intriguing shadows to the art. "You weren't well, and I..."

"Wasn't confident," he whispered, pulling his shirt on and covering what she could have stared at all day.

Bella took a step back, smoothing her hands down the front of her satin nightgown. "Not that you'd want me to see you at your most vulnerable, no."

He turned and took her face in his palms. "Bella, *mie drago'va*, you are the only one I would ever allow to see me vulnerable."

Her heart fluttered. The intense gold of his eyes seemed to blaze. She wrapped her hands around his wrists and took a deep breath.

Bang, bang, bang!

"Hello! Ralstons? I'm afraid we're running quite behind this morning. Is everything all right in there?" Leander's muffled voice sounded from the door. Another quick succession of knuckle raps on the door. "Hello? We're already late for our appointment at the Museum of History."

Growling, Markus dropped his hands. He pivoted on his heels and stalked to the door. Yanking it open, he left, the slam cutting off the angry bite of his words. Bella exhaled on a heavy huff. Lunah stretched out her front paws, her tail in the air, and whined.

"Yeah, me too," Bella agreed.

She went through her morning hygiene routine quickly and threw on the first matching pieces of clothing she pulled from her bag. A flowy pair of lemon-yellow pants and a white tunic top with navy and yellow flowers. While containing her curls on top of her head with a clip, Bella hunted for her shoes. She found them by the bed and smiled at the memory of Markus taking care of her the day before.

Sitting on the mussed bed, she squeezed her legs closed for a moment as tendrils of unsatisfied lust thrummed through her. She'd been somewhat sexually frustrated in the past with Markus when their kissing had gone farther than any kiss she'd ever experienced before. But this morning... *nothing* compared to the wild desire she'd felt for her husband. If they'd been interrupted even five minutes later? They'd have been walked in on, she knew it, because neither of them would have cared enough to stop. The thought made another shiver of need race through her.

Bella slipped on her shoes. Lunah stood waiting by the door while Bella grabbed her messenger bag. She emptied out the items she'd used during traveling, lessening her load and creating room for anything she'd need to collect along the investigation. The corridor was empty when she left the room. On the way to the stairs, she took in all the vivid colors and cultural touches so foreign to her, from the pattern worked into the runner rug to the geometric shapes and animals painted on the tiles hung from the walls.

Voices floated up the stairs. The deepest one she recognized among the three, and she smiled. Her husband's unique timbre sent warmth through her body. Lunah raced down the steps, a high-pitched yip echoing out behind her, behaving like she'd gone weeks without her alpha instead of only minutes. Though Bella could relate. Anticipation made her heart race and her steps quicker. Markus waited for her at the bottom. He wrapped her in a tight hug the second he could reach her.

Bella laughed. "I guess we all missed each other."

He took her lips in a long, deep kiss that left them both breathless when he finally ended the embrace. "I have spent enough time away from you."

Wasn't that the truth. He took a step back, lacing their fingers together. "Are you hungry?"

"Actually, I am," she said, surprised she just now felt the pangs of an empty stomach.

A wiry man with midnight skin stepped forward and offered her a small basket. A bright yellow shirt was tucked into loose white pants. Long lengths of sheer fabric formed a sash around his waist in maroon, sage green, and slate blue, fluttering from his left hip down past his knee. "Food for the beauty."

Bella flushed and accepted the basket. Behind him, Leander made odd motions, bringing his hand to his chest and bowing. He repeated the process and waved at the man.

"Oh! Um…" Bella mimicked Leander's movements. "Thank you."

"Most welcome. Enjoy." After bowing, the man picked up a watering can and began tending to the large collection of plants arranged around the bottom floor.

Leander adjusted his shoulder bag, then his glasses, and waved at the door. "May we leave for the museum now?"

Outside, a warm breeze teased Leander's mop and kicked up dust along their shoes. Bella dug into the basket, removing a sticky braided length of fried dough. She took a test taste and was pleasantly surprised by the sweet citrus flavor with a hint of floral spice she couldn't place. Meat on a stick was also in the basket and a small clay bowl of red berries. Markus grabbed the meat, offered her a bite, and then took one himself. Savory garlic and spice exploded across her tongue and she pressed honeyed fingers to her mouth to keep from moaning.

"Is all the food like this?" she asked, taking another bite of bread.

Leander nodded. "Mmm, yes, mostly. There are entire shops dedicated to nothing but spices and herbs here. Hundreds of them. They use them to flavor everything."

Bella examined the braided pastry, shiny with sweetness. She took another bite. "I don't know what I'm going to do when we get home. Our food isn't nearly this flavorful."

"I can tell you where some fantastic bakers are. You live near many of them, in Extilis Square," Leander said, guiding them down the street.

The midmorning sun gleamed between

single and two-story buildings, casting long shadows across the sidewalk. Lampposts were positioned every few feet, decorated by square planters at their bases overflowing with blooming vines in a rainbow of colors. The sandy shade of all the buildings and the brick road made the pigments even more vivid. Shutters were painted in bright, happy hues, as were doors, breaking up the monotony of the mason's work. Bella took it all in while eating her breakfast.

Around them, the city bustled. Women rushed by with baskets clutched in their hands loaded with fabric or food goods. Long streamers of various colors of material flowed from a metal band secured to their left bicep. The color didn't seem to have anything to do with the clothing they wore, some a complete contrast that had Bella taking a second look. The men wore the multi-colored sashes like their host.

"What are the bands and belts for?" Bella asked.

"Family colors," Leander answered. "They're also tied at a tomb when a family member dies."

He pointed to something far in the distance and Bella stopped, shading her eyes. A huge monolithic structure rose from the desert, reaching high into the sky. Rectangular in shape, with gaping openings between floors, the structure reminded her of something she'd once seen in a museum, but she couldn't place what.

"That's how they tend to their dead?"

"Yes. Vertical cemeteries. The only culture I know that does so."

Every country seemed to have a different way of handling their deceased. Sziveria cremated and buried the remains as deep as possible once the permafrost thawed. Entire families could be placed in the same small area. Italyssa sent their loved ones out into the ocean with great fanfare. Westica differed by region, from casket burials in the ground to casket burials in stone structures above the ground. Bella had never heard of a vertical cemetery, and to see one was quite an experience. She wanted to go closer and investigate.

"Can we visit them?" she asked.

"Sure." Leander offered a weak smile over his shoulder. "Perhaps Oberon will even be able to go along and give you a bit of a history lesson. I only know nothing is allowed to be built taller than the cemeteries."

Markus took her hand after she wiped it clean and squeezed her fingers. They continued, weaving along streets for blocks until they reached a soaring archway that led to a long, bricked walkway flanked by trees and shrubbery. The sidewalk led to a circular garden, where three white pillared buildings curved around the open space. They passed under the arch and headed to the gardens. Birds fluttered and sang from the tree branches above them. Squirrels chased each other down trunks and across the walkways.

Leander waved at several people carrying books and folders between the buildings. Banners hung from the top floor to the lowest, each a different color with words in a language Bella didn't understand. They fluttered in the wind, the sound of heavy fabric snapping joined the rustle of leaves and wildlife. There were no vehicles or horses or angry pedestrians shouting. City sounds were replaced with the tranquility of an academic campus. Bella wanted to sit and simply exist in the peaceful solitude offered.

A coppice of trees off to the right behind one of the buildings provided a sense of seclusion. Lunah bounded off to the miniature woods, a happy bounce in her steps.

"She needs to stretch and run," Markus said. "I only let her out long enough to prevent accidents through the night."

Something Bella had slept right through. "I'm sure she's more than excited to explore a new forest."

Leander led them into the center building. Inside, Thanzia Museum of History was carved into a large slate stone in multiple languages in the center of the lobby. More banners hung from the ceiling. Skylights and expansive windows let in natural light. All three floors were visible from ground level. White stone railings wrapped around each floor, and stairs were available in several places.

Leander went to a wide staircase on the right. "Oberon's colleagues and office are on the second floor, in the west wing."

Bella wanted Oberon to be in his office, distracted by his exciting find. Yes, that would mean their trip was for nothing, but it'd also mean Leander's friend was safe and well. Bella wanted that for the quirky academic.

"Is Lunah okay?" Bella asked Markus, whispering. He still held her hand and thankfully, the stairs were wide enough to accommodate them and others.

"She's fine. Hunting a squirrel. The little beasties look different than ours."

Bella tried to recall what the rodents had looked like, racing each other outside. "Not as fluffy."

"And striped." He smiled. "That's my favorite part of traveling, all the differences."

Leander disappeared down a corridor to the right and they hustled to catch up. Mirrors were hung in strategic positions to reflect natural and gas lamp lights. The lamps were artistic glass rectangles with thin brass frames holding the panes in place. Brass guards behind the flames produced a warm glow along the walls painted neutral.

At an office door, Leander bounced on his feet. He motioned, his body tight with impatience, his mouth a thin line.

"Your friend will not be found faster by us running into his office," Markus stated.

Leander twitched his nose, making his pencil-thin mustache dance. "I know, I'm just anxious to go inside, and I don't want to accidentally disturb any potential evidence."

"You won't hurt anything going inside first," Bella said.

Nodding, Leander opened the door and then stumbled back.

Markus halted Bella. "Wait, let me see what's going on."

She released his hand. "Go ahead, let me know when to join you."

He glanced around the wide hall as if a threat would spring from the wall before nodding and brushing past Leander to enter the office. Seconds later, he poked his head out and waved for her. Bella braced herself for whatever had negatively affected Leander and entered a disaster. The room couldn't have been more disheveled if a wind storm had swept through. Covered in loose papers, nothing of the floor was visible. Most of the shelves were bare, a few haphazard books were toppled over like loose teeth. Objects littered the desk, from books to small, broken clay pieces. Bella wondered if the fragments were already busted or if someone had destroyed a priceless piece of history in their obvious efforts to find something.

Markus picked a few sheets up from the desk. "This will take us hours to search through, and we still may not know what they were looking for."

Leander hesitated at the door and didn't move over the threshold. "Probably information on his discovery."

Bella looked over the tossed room. "I don't think they found anything."

Leander took a tentative step in. "How can you tell?"

Markus set the papers down, his attention on her. Heat suffused her cheeks. "Whoever did this was angry."

"Yes," Markus agreed quietly, glancing around. "That fits."

Leander shoved a hand into his wild hair. "If they were angry enough to destroy his workplace, what must they have done to him? How will we ever learn what's happened to him?" He kicked his toes into the clutter on the floor. Papers fluttered up, and a chunk of stone skittered across the room. "I mean, look at this. Look at what someone did to all his hard work. They obviously didn't care about all his research or the historical advances he'd helped this country make or—"

"Mr. Kavont," Markus said sternly. "There is nobody here. Your friend may be fine, or he may be in trouble. We don't know. Getting upset before we have any answers helps nothing. Do you know where he lives?"

Leander blinked, his eyes huge behind his glasses. "Um, I'm not certain, but we can find someone who worked with him who should."

"Let's have that be our second place to search. Maybe we'll find some answers there," Markus said.

Nodding, Leander moved from the entrance back into the hall. Markus followed. Alone, Bella touched a broken clay bowl with remnants of pale gray, soft brown, and slate-painted leaf patterns. Or perhaps it had been a vase and resembled a bowl now. Either way, the piece was beautiful in its simplicity. She hoped someone was able to preserve what remained. Oberon Rima cared about the history he'd uncovered. The treasures he provided for a people to learn about where they came from. Who they'd once been. That someone had felt they had the right to come into this space and destroy not only the lifework of a man but the very story of humanity angered her. She hoped a colleague cared enough to collect and reorganize the office if the worst had come to pass for the archeologist.

She closed the door with a low click. The hall was quiet and empty, except for Markus, who leaned against the wall, arms crossed, waiting for her. Straightening from the wall, he motioned with his head for her to follow. Bella grabbed the messenger bag strap in both hands and trailed after him.

Markus stopped in front of a wall facing a bank of windows. Ten paintings were hung in a row to take full advantage of the light. He pointed at the third one from the left. Beneath the image of a man with styled dark blond hair, sun-darkened skin, and sky-blue eyes was the name Oberon Rima and his impressive academic credentials, along with his position within the department. A smile displayed even white teeth and made his gaze sparkle at the viewer.

Bella touched the bottom corner of the frame. "I want very much for this man to be alive."

Markus took her hand and squeezed. "We will do everything we can to find him."

Rapid footsteps echoed from the left. Bella raised her eyebrows and leaned forward to see. Leander rushed toward them, a paper fluttering in his upheld hand.

"I have it!" he proclaimed, lifting the sheet higher. "I have Oberon's address. We can go. Right now."

The historian breezed past, his cream jacket fluttering out behind him.

Markus shook his head but followed. "Hopefully, our next location will provide more answers."

SIX

"Here we are." Leander pointed at a three-story sandstone structure. A stairwell in the center led to the upper floors, with a door on each side. Leander consulted the paper and pointed again. "Oberon is apartment 3b."

"What about a key?" Bella asked, coming to stand beside him.

"Oh, uh." Leander scratched his head and scrunched his nose. "I'm not sure about that."

"We'll check to see if he hid one somewhere. If not, I can handle it," Markus said. "Let's go before we attract unwanted attention."

Lunah trailed after Markus on the stairs. Bella brought up the end of their little line. At the door, Markus searched the frame under a doormat and the windowsill of the closest window. When none of them turned up a key, he dug inside his jacket until he found a multiuse tool he always kept on hand. He isolated the proper utensil and then went to work on the knob. The quiet *snick* of the lock opening made him smile. He pressed the door open and waited for the group to enter ahead of him. Before closing the door, he checked to ensure their little break-and-enter had gone unnoticed.

The apartment showed no signs of anyone having beaten them to the premises. Books were stacked neatly on almost every surface. Maps, sketches of historical objects, paintings of civilizations before the cataclysm, and small artifacts framed in shadow boxes covered almost every inch of wall space. Documents overloaded a desk positioned near a window. Leander made a beeline for the desk and started sifting through the papers. Bella went to the nearest wall and studied the pieces. Markus smiled at his beautiful, inquisitive mate.

"No one has been here," Leander said in relief. He lifted some papers and shifted more around. "Look at these sketches, and here are some recent notes, and, oh! I think this is his field journal."

"I wonder if someone was looking for his apartment key in his office, and when they didn't find it, destroyed everything," Markus said, picking up a few books to look at the spines. They were written in various languages, of which he only recognized one. He returned them to the stack and went through a small dining and kitchen combination to a doorway. "I'm going to look in his bedroom."

Picking his way through the modest space, he found the nearest window and opened the curtain. The light revealed rumpled blankets, an indented pillow, more books stacked on the nightstand, and a dresser with a drawer left open. Markus always hated this part of an investigation. Walking into a life placed on pause, where the person had had no idea they'd never return home. The invasion of privacy seemed somehow more profound.

After checking the dresser, he respectfully closed all the drawers and went to the nightstand. He sat on the bed and opened the top drawer. The usual objects of a man were tossed in haphazardly. A quick shift of contents revealed nothing important. He moved on to the stack of books. Since bedside reading was usually more important, Markus flipped through the pages to check for anything hidden between pages or marked that could help them in their search.

Two books surprised him, not having been research material at all but rather imaginative drawings meant to entice and arouse. He snapped those closed quickly. Markus didn't need any help in *that* area of his life right now, thank you very much. The memory of Bella willing beneath his touch, of the incredible way her tight and slick opening had nearly welcomed him inside, had him fidgeting in discomfort to adjust the stiffness in his pants.

He found a stack of journals on the bottom shelf of the stand. The top diary had a date from three weeks ago. He searched backward, noting the dates were regular. Oberon never skipped more than two days between entries. That he'd missed three entire weeks? Dread settled like a heavy stone in his stomach. Not a positive development. Sighing, Markus snapped the leather binding closed and hung his head. He'd have to deliver the bad news to Leander.

Journals in hand, Markus returned to the living room. Bella was at the desk helping Leander place folders, files, envelopes, and loose sheets of paper into a small box. Lunah lounged along a thick beam of sun. Bella noticed him first, her hands pausing mid-drop to the box.

"You found something," she said quietly.

"I did," he said, shifting his attention to Leander. He held out the top journal. "I'm so sorry."

Hands trembling, Leander accepted the diary. He did the same thing Markus had, checked the dates, but unlike Markus, he went to the beginning and requested another. Markus handed the next one over and waited for Leander to accept the dreadful truth.

The chance of Oberon Rima coming home was slim.

Leander stumbled over to a blanket-draped couch, collapsing on the cushions. Shoulders hunched, he dropped both the journals onto his lap and stared down at them. "I can't... I can't believe this. Do you..." He licked his lips. "Do you think he's dead?"

Markus handed Bella the other diaries and then crouched before the dejected historian. He touched a hand to Leander's knee and waited for the man's sad gaze to lift. "The odds are no longer in his favor to be found safe."

"What do we do now?" he whispered.

"I don't know the legal system here. Do we report a missing person?" Markus asked.

Leander shook his head and then brought his

hands up the side of his face. "No, there are no police. There are magistrates of a sort, but a wrongdoing is brought before them along with all the evidence. They'll decide if they'll interview anyone and bring a conviction. Punishment here for even the simplest crimes is harsh, so the culture is mostly crimeless."

Markus glanced at Bella, who shrugged helplessly. He wished he could speak to her as he did Lunah and find out if she wanted to help or tell Leander they'd done what they'd come to Thanzia to do— discover if his friend was missing. He hoped if she were to choose differently, she'd forgive him.

"What do you wish to do, Mr. Kavont?" Markus asked.

Leander wiped the back of his hand under his nose, sniffling. "I need to know what happened to him."

Markus dropped his head and sighed. "Of course. This may take some time."

"If the museum won't cover your fee, I will. I'm more than capable," Leander said quickly.

Bella's gentle hand laid on Markus's shoulder and squeezed. Markus brushed her fingers in acknowledgment and because he needed the contact. Even in the same room, he missed her. Seemed she did as well, for she slid her hand to his neck, beneath his hair.

"We aren't worried about that, Leander," she said.

Markus pressed his lips closed. They were a team, and showing a unified front was important. However, he'd remind her they had an apartment to furnish back in their room.

"Thank you," Leander rasped. "But I will still pay your fee and all expenses while we're here. It's only fair."

"Thank *you*," Markus said before Bella could reply. "We appreciate that."

Leander held the journals out to Markus. "What is the next step?"

Bella reached over and took the journals. "We'll look over everything we've found here."

"His journals may be a big help in revealing what was going on in his life before his disappearance," Markus said.

Leander rubbed his face with both his hands, dislodging his glasses. "Maybe he revealed where the site is. Out here, in the desert, things remain preserved." He sat up straighter, his glasses still crooked. "Maybe there will be something to find, some sort of clue."

"Maybe," Markus said. "If whoever ransacked his office also knew where to find the site. Right now, we only know Oberon is indeed missing."

Leander sighed. "All right. If I tell the museum we're also looking for the site along with the archeologist, and I can get the lead historian here in Lagosin to agree to joint credit and allow me to take a few artifacts home for Sziverian's museums, then I know they'll continue to cover expenses."

"Do you think Oberon's colleagues will want to know what happened enough to agree to that arrangement?" Bella asked.

Leander fixed his glasses and nodded. "If

Oberon was telling the truth about his discovery? Absolutely. They'll have so many artifacts that taking a box full for our society to view and learn from won't be missed. And they'll be on loan anyway. An actual, preserved section of a pre-cataclysm city will bring tourism and become a cultural treasure trove for Thanzia. Only a handful of countries can offer such."

Markus only knew of one for certain, and that was Miami Island. The remnants of steel and glass buildings and huge metal cylinders once believed to fly in the sky were conserved for people to explore and learn about past human life. He had to admit that he was curious about what Oberon may have found and if it compared to what Miami Island boasted.

"We'll let you know if we find anything useful," Bella said. "We packed up everything on his desk. Do you know of anywhere else he may have kept notes?"

"No," Leander said, shaking his head. "I doubt he knew he ever had to worry about being cautious." He raised a hand in bewilderment. "I mean, whoever would have thought archaeology was dangerous?"

"Looters, a rival colleague, or someone who just didn't like what he'd found, or maybe it's completely unrelated to the excavating," Markus said. "Maybe Oberon was already in trouble, and you just didn't know it."

Nervous flutters tingled in Bella's stomach as she followed behind Markus to their room.

They'd parted ways with Leander after they finished at the apartment, the academic being too anxious to wait to speak with the Director of History at the museum. Bella wanted to get started on the box of evidence, but she wanted her husband more. And they'd be alone for at least an hour, if not longer before Leander would interrupt. Bella was determined to make use of the time. She just needed to find the same courage she'd had this morning.

Markus unlocked their room and held the door open for her and Lunah. The space had been freshened, and a bowl of water, meat, and potatoes was on the floor in the living space. Lunah sat at the offerings and looked at Markus. He picked up both and moved them into the bathroom, closing the door after the wolf. Bella raised a brow and set the box on the low table.

He stopped at the end of the short hall, his eyes burning. "Come here, mate."

Yes.

Nervousness melted into need, and Bella didn't hesitate. She launched at him, sending him tumbling backward into the room's door. He hoisted her up, his hands gripping her rear in an almost painful grasp. Bella squeezed her thighs around his hips and grabbed his chin to catch his mouth. He opened, and his tongue glided along hers.

Throwing off any shyness, Bella yanked first at his braid, loosening the thick fall of hair down his back, and then she tugged at his shirt. With creative maneuvering, he somehow kept her latched to his frame while removing the clothing.

The second her fingers touched the warmth of his bare skin, she couldn't stop a moan from escaping. Her hands slid across the shifting muscles of his shoulders and into the weight of his hair.

Markus spun them into the right wall, bracing her against the rough textured surface while he removed her top with trembling hands. Bella helped, shaking the fabric free of her arm. The course plaster bit into her back, but she barely noticed, her awareness focused on her husband's revealed chest. She pressed her palms against his pecs, caressing along the muscles and the fine dusting of hair. He lifted a leg, taking her weight on his thigh, leaving his hands free to roam her stomach, sides, and breasts.

Bella's eyes fluttered closed as he found one, then the other breast, lavishing attention with his hands and mouth. Delicate yet intense sensations raced through her body straight to her core. She'd never imagined her modest breasts would not only be something he'd desire but something she'd enjoy having attention paid to. He sucked, nipped, licked, and somehow managed to make her forget she didn't have much to offer. Once before, he'd given her a sample of what to expect in his bed. Time had dulled the memory, and as he bit gently on her sensitive nipple, she couldn't wait any longer to discover what they'd had to put on hold for too many long months.

Squirming, she reached between their bodies and fumbled with the top button of his pants. His mouth moved to her neck, then her jaw, and up to her lips, where his kiss distracted her. Her hands left his pants to grasp his shoulders, holding him tight. His tongue explored every inch of her mouth and tangled with hers, drawing her deeper into a haze of lust. Distracting to the point that she didn't even realize they'd moved until her back slammed into the mattress.

Cold air rushed over her torso, and her grumble of irritation turned to a gasp as her pants were yanked from her legs. She barely had time to register the shocking exposure before he grabbed her knees, parted her thighs, and dove his face between them.

"Markus!" Bella yelped.

She grabbed fistfuls of his hair with the intent of shoving him away, only to hold tight when his tongue licked from her clit to her opening and speared deep. Her hips arched, and she gave a startled cry of pleasure. What was he doing to her? She couldn't think, form a single legible word, or do much more than writhe as pleasure built until she thought she'd burst. And still, she needed... more.

"S-stop," she gasped, pulling harder on his hair. "I want... need... please...."

Growling, he crawled up her body. The harsh light spilling in from the two open windows illuminated his masculine form. Unlike this morning, when he'd been completely hidden from her sight, there was no mistaking his member's erect, heavy state or how very much he desired her. Moisture gleamed from the tip, and Bella had a moment of equal parts alarm and anticipation. She *needed* to know how he'd feel moving inside her, and at the same time, she seriously doubted his ability to fit.

Uncertainty must have shown on her face, for he braced himself on his elbow and grasped her face. His hard length pressed into her belly. He kissed her gently. Once, twice, soft teasing kisses that made her sigh and relax. She grasped his wrists and drew her knees to his hips, cradling him between her legs.

"I will go slow," he whispered against her lips.

Bella shook her head. "I don't want slow."

"But—"

She squeezed his wrists and met his confused stare. Oh, he had such beautiful eyes. "I've never done this before."

"I know, that's why—"

"But," she quickly cut in before she lost her courage, "I won't hurt like a virgin. Not really."

He straightened his arms, looming above her, the confusion deepening across his handsome face. "What do you mean?"

Heat prickled across her cheeks. Would she be able to confess her dirty little secret? Bella brushed long strands of hair behind his ears, her gaze searching his. Perhaps, to him, it wouldn't be so dirty. And they certainly shouldn't have any secrets. She took a deep breath and, on the exhale, admitted to her erotic midnight pastime. Or rather, her carnal fantasies that had led to her not being a typical innocent.

"I wasn't great at it," she conceded softly. "But I enjoyed how I could make myself feel. And

I liked trying to imagine what we'd be like. How we'd fit. How you'd move inside me."

His hand slid between their bodies and touched her clit, to her slick core and back up, making her throb. He pressed two fingers deep, pumped them, and pulled them free, repeating the agonizing teasing. Desire brightened his already near-glowing golden eyes. "Using a small glass intimate toy?"

She squirmed, panting. "Yes."

He leaned close, his lips brushing her ear, his hair creating a curtain obscuring the world. "That'll be fun when we return home," he breathed.

And then he was pressing inside her. Stretching her, retreating, moving deeper, rolling his hips, and helping her angle her own until he could go no further, seated completely. Bella tilted her head back and stared at the ceiling, gasping, her inner muscles contracting from the foreign sensation. He nipped and kissed her neck. Slow at first, he tested their joined state, thrusting in shallow increments.

"Okay?" he asked, one hand gripping her thigh while the other wrapped around her shoulder from underneath, anchoring her.

Bella wiggled and took stock of the faint burn that faded into pleasure with each gradual retreat that was returned with a harder plunge. *Oh yes...* She dug her nails into his hip and backside, pulling her knees tighter. "More."

He complied, driving harder, moving faster. Bella demanded even more, bucking beneath him, meeting each forceful slam of his hips.

Sharp cries escaped her with each strong thrust, a familiar quest to achieve ecstasy-filled heights. Intensified by the fact that she wasn't alone, and he was so, *so* much better than any foreign object. She knew she was being unreasonable in her demands. He couldn't feasibly go any faster or sink into her deeper, but she pleaded for the impossible. Euphoria crashed through her like a tidal wave, locking her muscles, robbing her voice, and causing her spine to bow. At the highest rise, she managed a choked scream, an incoherent plea that she not experience the moment alone.

Markus didn't deny her. He jerked forward, groaned, and heat poured into her. Lightning sizzled along her nerves, and her body matched his fierce tremble. Another shocking swell of pleasure coursed through her body.

Long moments passed before either of them could move in the aftermath. Sweaty, breathless, loose-limbed, Bella lay sprawled beneath his weight. He stirred first. Groaning, he shifted off her. The sudden loss of him pulling out made her squeal. He laughed, kissed her nose, and rose way faster than should be possible. Bella lifted onto her elbows and admired his retreating form, the stunning ink and tight backside making her bite her bottom lip. Yep, that was all hers now. Completely.

Tendrils of awareness still pulsed from her core. Curious, she reached down, touched herself, and grimaced at the wet, swollen mess she encountered.

"Here," Markus whispered, making her jump.

She snatched her hand away and clamped

her legs closed. He'd knelt at the foot of the bed, a washcloth in hand. Grabbing her left calf, he pulled her to the edge of the mattress.

"Don't be shy now," he teased, half smiling.

Bella pressed her lips together and wrapped her arms around her waist. She remained quiet as he gently parted her thighs and cleaned her. The damp cloth felt good against her heated flesh. He kissed the inside of her leg.

"Only a little blood. How do you feel?" he asked.

How to answer that? Somewhat mortified, he'd caught her exploring the post-sex condition of her body. Wholly sated from his toe-curling ability to bring her to orgasm. Sore because she'd demanded more than she should have her first time, and he'd indulged, making her even more excited for the future in their bed. All these thoughts clamored in her mind, leaving her speechless.

Markus laughed and laid his head on her thigh, leaving the cloth over her mound. "No words, huh? I was that good?"

Bella joined his laughter, covering her eyes with her arm. "I don't know what to say... I feel great. And a little embarrassed, and, yes. I'm okay."

The damp fabric disappeared, and the bed dipped beneath his weight. His touch caressed from her hip to her side, resting around her ribs under her breast. "Do you want to nap or get started on the case?"

She shifted her arm above her head and blinked up at him. He'd tied his hair back into a loose ponytail and had pulled on his pants. She still lay completely naked and couldn't muster up the energy to care for the moment.

"We should probably work on the case, don't you think? Leander will ask if we've made any progress after he speaks to whoever he needed to at the museum," she said, stretching her arms above her.

His gaze darkened, and he looked her over, from her breasts tilted toward him to her pointed toes. She couldn't help the little arch of her spine and twist of her hips under his attention. His hand tightened on her side.

"*Krahet'sna,* you keep tempting me, and we won't be doing much of anything useful," he growled.

"I tempt you?" she asked.

He kissed her, long and deep, and only when she was grasping at his bare shoulders, wanting him all over again, did he stop and whisper against her mouth, "Always."

Warmth spread through her, and she hugged him. "All right, I'll be good. Then we can let Lunah out, too."

He shifted enough to let her rise and scoot to the end of the bed. She didn't get far. He grabbed her arm with a shout of Ruthenian she couldn't decipher. Alarmed, she glanced over her shoulder to find him staring at her wide-eyed.

Panic replaced her happy glow. "What is it? What's wrong?"

CHAPTER

SEVEN

Markus didn't know how to tell her. While excitement and possession made him want to snatch her to his chest and hold her tight, apprehension over how she'd react kept him frozen.

Behind the bathroom door, Lunah yipped, having picked up on his strong reaction. *She is your true mate, she is!*

Markus ran a hand down his face. *Dak.* Yes.

"Markus," Bella said, her voice tense. "What is it? Tell me."

"We are... mated," he said quietly.

She lifted her brows. "Yes, I know. I was there."

Markus sat up and took her hand in both of his. "No. It's more than our coming together, it's—"

How did he describe something so common in his land but completely foreign to her? He closed his eyes and searched for the thread he should have known before this moment. So lost in how good she'd felt wrapped around him, her pleasure ricocheting through him, he'd missed the moment he'd fully bonded. Bella had the ability to do that to him, make him lose all sanity. Like a length of cord in his mind anchoring him to his wife, he found the tie that bound. He sent his worry and his hope to her.

"Whoa!" she exclaimed, her free hand rising in alarm. "Whoa, whoa... what was that?"

Markus' hand tightened around hers. "That was... me."

She pulled free and tucked tangled curls behind her ears. "You? What do you mean?"

"Ruthenian's bond for life," he told her.

"Yes, I remember you telling me such."

"Each couple is different, their bond unique like their relationship. But beast masters, we're on a different level entirely," he explained. "We bond in a similar manner like with our animal."

She stood and held her hands out again. "I need to get dressed for this conversation."

Markus grabbed her arm, stopping her. "Wait. There's something you need to see first."

He guided her to the bathroom, trying to ignore the soft bounce of her small, unbound breasts and the supple sway of her hips. She was slender, her legs long, her stomach flat, her hips flared, and her rear big enough to fill both his palms. The bright afternoon sun made her pale brown skin glow, and the damp curls between her legs glisten. She was a walking temptation.

"You're scaring me," she whispered, avoiding their discarded shoes strewn across the floor. Markus didn't even remember removing and throwing them.

"I don't mean to, but this is important." He

opened the bathroom door. Lunah pounced out and went to investigate their scattered clothing. Markus lit two of the lamps and then motioned to the mirror.

Bella shrugged, glancing at herself in the mirror and meeting his stare in the reflection. "What?

Markus gathered her loose curls and slid them over her shoulder. He kissed the base of her neck and then angled her enough to reveal the wolf tattoo covering her entire back. She gasped, swung her hips around, and tried to reach behind herself to touch the intricate artwork.

"What in the artic?" she breathed. "How...."

Markus traced the lines of the art he'd seen fully once, right before it'd been transferred to his back, and a needle had worked ink into his flesh. "It's a mystery of my genetics. Only beast masters have this ability."

"I didn't feel anyth— no, wait, I did... like when lightning strikes too close," she said, reaching over her shoulder to brush the tips of the wolf's ears. "Everything tingled. Incredible."

"You aren't upset?" He caught her gaze in the mirror again.

She turned and wrapped her arms around his neck, rising on her tiptoes to kiss him. Her breasts brushed his bare chest, and he swallowed a groan. "I didn't know exactly what being with you would involve, but I knew it would be different. No one will see this mark but you. It's something special between us."

He held onto her hips, rocking his. "Not true

in Ruthenia. Beast masters show off their mated bond in public."

Laughing, she twirled her fingers into the loose hair from his ponytail between his shoulder blades. "If we end up in Ruthenia for a visit, I will proudly display your mark."

For a visit. Because they couldn't make their home in his motherland. When he'd set foot on a ship heading for Sziveria and his wife, he'd left behind the only home he'd ever known. His country's inability to accept those with any genetically common genes meant his mate and, subsequently, their children would be shunned. A future he was unwilling to put those he loved through.

Yes, he loved her. Had for some time but hadn't been willing to tell her over the radio, and there'd been no moments since his chaotic arrival. Now, with her naked in his arms, he didn't want her to feel pressured to express something she may not be ready for. The right moment would happen, or he'd blurt it out when he could no longer contain himself.

Markus hugged her tight, his hands splaying across her back over the claim that would forever mark her as his. No going back for either of them. He met his stare in the mirror, encountering a possessive side to his nature he hadn't seen before.

"What's wrong?" she asked, leaning back, her hands braced on his shoulders.

"You mean everything to me," he whispered.

Her fingers brushed across his beard. "I—"

A heavy thump sounded next door. Markus

touched his forehead to hers, sighing. He reached behind the linens hanging on the wall and handed her a thin robe. Leander had a habit of interrupting at the most inopportune moment, and if he saw Markus's bride in any state of undress, Markus would have to hurt the academic. Best to eliminate the temptation.

Bella shrugged into the teal cotton, hiding all her delicious skin from view. Including his mating mark. Markus sighed again. The traditional open-backed attire of his homeland made so much more sense, with a mate bearing his mark. He wanted her nudity hidden. What stated they were paired? Not so much.

Holding the edges closed, Bella smiled up at him. "Any other surprises for me?"

Markus stepped out of the bathroom and shrugged. "I have no idea. I'm as brand new to this as you are. There may be some surprises for me, too."

She went into the living area, picking up discarded clothing. At the couch, she sat and began to pull on her pants while peering into the box containing the evidence from Oberon's apartment. "Not much of what we found was written in Atlantic."

"I noticed that as well." He sat adjacent to her on an overstuffed armchair. "But we'll still be able to learn a lot about his life."

She stood long enough to discard the robe and pull her tunic back on. Markus swallowed and turned his attention to the box, trying to ignore knowing that she wore absolutely nothing under the clothes. No chemise, no panties. Her clothes were always a bit too big for her, hiding her figure.

But Markus knew what she had to offer.

Her curves may be modest, but they were breathtaking in every way. Her breasts were perfect for his mouth, her nipples a rich chocolate brown. The flat plane of her stomach had guided his attention to what rested between her thighs. Bliss. Her hips and thighs full. Pliant. Accepting his rough need to hold, to submit, to guide. Markus wanted to do it all again, in different ways, with the same result. Both of them winded, sweaty, and sated. He'd never had such a sense of anticipation with a lover before. Then again, he'd never been in love before and been able to express his emotions in a physical act that had meaning for the first time.

Dressed, she tossed the robe over the back of the couch and returned to the box. She looked over each book, setting a few to the side and stacking the others closer to him. Some loose papers made it to her small pile, the rest she left in the box. Markus settled deep into the chair, spreading his arms wide over the armrests. This was his favorite part. When she became lost in the research, learning all the nuances of the person and their situation, he could never hope to see.

BELLA SET another drawing off to the side in a growing stack of similar renditions, something familiar about the three-story, basic rectangle structure nagging at her mind. She'd sorted a handful of such depictions, a reoccurring theme amongst Oberon's research. Unable to place why the decayed, often crumbling ruins tugged at a hidden memory, she returned to the books and notes written in Atlantic. Oberon seemed inclined to switch between languages based on what he used for research material. It was a quirky habit she hoped she'd be able to ask him about. Sadly, she had the feeling she never would.

"Did he tell anyone about his find?" Markus asked, closing a book and reaching for another.

"I can't tell. He wrote his journals in— it's not Thanzian. I'm not sure what language."

"He wrote the dates in Atlantic. Maybe it's his own personal code?"

Bella studied the words. "Maybe. The letters used are familiar in shape, but they have strange accents and don't spell any words I know."

Papers fluttered as he shifted through a small stack. "Maybe Leander will know."

"It's so odd," she mused, picking up a drawing again that troubled her. "Why write your diary in something no one would know?"

"Maybe he had issues with his research being stolen."

"Or his privacy being violated in some other manner." Bella shook her head. They could play this guessing game until they ran out of what-ifs. Only Oberon knew the truth.

Picking up the drawings, Bella wandered to the nearest window. The azure shutters were open, and a soft breeze fluttered the bright red and yellow curtains and teased the rainbow of flowers in hanging clay pots. Bella stared out over the landscape, taking in the sparse collection of trees that popped up between short clay buildings. The blue, cloudless horizon stretched for miles, broken by the occasional vertical cemetery and jagged mountain peaks. The papers crinkled as she rested her forearms on the sill and searched for... something.

Squinting against the sun sinking to her right, Bella looked over the quiet city below. Empty carts ambled by, pulled by slow donkeys, their owners walking alongside. Men and women carried baskets heaped with fabric or bags laden with goods. Children raced in the dusty streets, clattering sticks and using them to send balls rolling in every direction, their laughter joining the tranquil rush of wind. The scene was so much more than the hustle and racket of Haven City. Clean, safe, and sunny.

Not that she'd ever felt unsafe in her home city, but she couldn't recall seeing children playing in the street. Not even in The Rows, where the roads were too narrow for cart traffic. Something about their internal culture kept playing in personal spaces. Perhaps because of the months spent indoors, a problem Thanzia didn't have to worry about. She wondered what other nations had a community ambiance.

Other nations....

Bella straightened, holding the drawings in front of herself. Beneath each sketch was a scrawled location written in Atlantic. Uconnland, Westica. 7th Street Ruins, Miami Island. Torikia, Cairo. Astana-tau, Vativarsa. The drawings were of similar structures all over the inhabited world. Old, pre-cataclysm ruins that all had the same shape and feel. They even seemed to have crumbled and become preserved in the same manner. She held one of the drawings up higher. Switched it with another. And another. Her gaze changed between the sketches and the vertical cemeteries visible over the shorter city.

"Oh, my stars," she whispered.

"What is it?" Markus asked behind her, making her jump.

"Look," she urged, holding two pages up side by side just underneath a cemetery. "They're almost exactly the same."

Markus took a sheet from her and held it out the same way. "Other countries have these same cemeteries?"

"No, these are ruins of what they called parking decks, or gar-garah... gara..." Her tongue became tangled on the foreign word as she tried to remember how she'd once heard a tour guide pronounce the space. She cleared her throat and tried again. "Garage."

"What were they used for?"

"Vehicle parking."

Markus turned the paper, following the motion with his head. "What do you feel is so significant about this?"

"Remember the history lesson Leander gave us?" When all he did was blink at her, she laughed, kissed him, and held up the papers. "Thanzia prides itself on being a *new* culture in a post-cataclysm world. Unlike Italyssa, Ruthenia, Sziveria, and pretty much everyone else in the remaining space habitable by humans, who trace their lineage and aspects of their culture back to other lands, Thanzia claims they simply *became*. They just were. They are of the land, and everything that has resulted since is new to the world."

Markus's gaze narrowed. "But that might not be the case?"

Bella shook her head. "No. Not if Oberon made connections with other worldwide cultures, and now he's found proof a culture existed here previously? That means the people of Thanzia did, in fact, come from somewhere, bringing their traditions or perhaps creating new ones from what remained of past residences. They have a shared origin story, like the rest of us."

Slowly, he handed the drawing back to her. "His theories had the potential to change the nation's history."

"Yes."

Glancing back at the cluttered table of research, he ran a hand down his face. "I need to get Leander. We can't get much further in this investigation without knowing exactly what Oberon was working on."

"I'm surprised he still hasn't knocked."

"Maybe it wasn't him we heard next door."

Bella raised her brows.

Markus spoke quick Ruthenian commands to Lunah on his way to the door. Bella wanted to rush after them but stopped herself, pressing her feet to the wood floor. The pair disappeared, the door closing behind them. Bella looked at the sketches still in her hand and then over her shoulder to the vertical cemeteries. She wondered if the archaeological discovery of a previous civilization or the anthropological theories caused Oberon's disappearance. Or something they had yet even to learn.

Moments later, the door opened, and Leander entered first. His eyes were swollen and red behind his glasses. His pencil-thin mustache twitched as he sniffled. He brushed a trembling hand through his curls, adding to the frizz from too much touching. Bella glanced at Markus, who frowned and shook his head.

"Bad news at the museum?" Bella asked.

"The director of history feels Oberon's disappearance is a direct result of him being injured or lost while at his supposed archaeological discovery, which the museum only manages once the site has been confirmed," Leander said, his voice weak.

"And the discovery hadn't been confirmed?" Bella asked, taking a seat as Leander did.

"No." Leander sniffled again. "Oberon didn't even share the coordinates with the museum, only a handful of objects he'd found, which could have been located anywhere in the desert. Or, as the director said, at any relic dealer at the port cities."

"He hadn't found anything new?" Markus asked, leaning against the wall across from them.

"Not based on what the director showed me. Some cobalt glass plates, a preserved painting of plains with silhouetted animals, and a bottle of some type of liquor in a language long dead." Leander dropped his head into his hands, his mop of curls flopping, and sniffled. "All things—" His voice cracked, and he tried again, "All things we've seen before in other locations that get passed around like treasures among collectors anywhere in the world."

"So, nothing unique," Bella said.

"No," Leander snuffled.

Markus crouched down. Lunah pressed her nose into his chest. He ruffled her ears and slid his hand down the back of her head to the thick fur at her neck before gently coaxing her away. She chuffed but padded her way into the sleeping area, sitting at one of the windows to look outside. Bella met his ominous stare, the sentiment reflected in her hollow stomach. She hated the sense of inevitable doom the case had suddenly taken.

"Oberon may have written something down he didn't share with his superiors. Not all hope is lost until we have his full story," Markus said quietly. "Will you help us?"

Lifting his head, Leander blinked his watery eyes. "Of course, absolutely. What are you needing help with?"

Bella held out Oberon's journals and the notes he'd written in languages she didn't understand. "We can't read any of these."

"All right, let me see if I can help. I don't speak as many languages as he did, but he did write to me in the same language he wrote for his diary," Leander said, accepting the journals as a stack and resting the lot of them on his thighs.

"What is it?" Bella asked.

"An early form of Atlantic. Our language has evolved since its first recorded iteration, as languages are apt to do. All professions involving history must learn it since all early PCE history is written in this form across several countries." He opened the top journal, closed it, and picked up the next one. "Let's see what he had to say in the weeks before his disappearance."

Leander turned pages, quietly reading to himself. A few times, he gasped, and Bella wanted to rush him to find out what he was learning. When he continued to read silently, she nudged his shoe with her bare toes. A subtle reminder they were waiting for his translation.

"Listen to this," Leander said, leaning forward, setting the other diaries aside. He pushed up his glasses before beginning, "Oberon is writing about the site, which he'd just uncovered. First, he'd found some broken glass, small rusted tubes of some kind, and odd metal coils near a fissure in the sand. When he investigated the small opening further, he found that it led to the buried site."

Leander then went on to read the entry directly. Both Bella and Markus leaned closer, becoming enthralled by the tale of unearthing woven in the journal in Oberon's words. For years, Oberon had hypothesized about the design of Thanzia's vertical cemeteries. They weren't original, but rather, in a post-cataclysmic world with limited resources and tools, early Thanzians had used a structure already in place to make handling their dead easier. The above-ground structures provided a simpler way than digging into the ground, and the endless supply of sand was a way to create bricks and mortar for body storage. The summer heat provided a means of slow, natural cremation, making the tombs reusable for generations of the same family.

He'd found proof in the earliest structures in areas of Thanzia that had since been abandoned. The parking decks had only lasted the inhabitants for a hundred or so years before needing to be built from new material. He'd done detailed sketches, taken measurements, and even found several areas where painted lines remained on the floors beneath the crumbling tombs.

Bella searched for the drawings among the evidence they'd collected. She thought she'd isolated all the parking garages but realized when she found the set she'd overlooked them due to the crypts in the drawings. She moved to the floor near Markus and laid them out in a row. A line jumped out at her at the bottom of the drawing.

"Look, there it is," she said.

Markus tapped his toes near another sketch. "Here, too, he recorded three of them between these five tombs."

Leander stood, the journal still in hand, his finger holding the place where he'd left off. "He says when he approached the museum board about his findings, they stated that the markings must have been used to measure how many graves could fit into a space. Oberon was looking for tangible proof the lines were, in fact, pre-cataclysmic. The paint was reflective in candle and natural light, something we do not use, but that wasn't enough for the board members and was rejected as confirmation."

Bella sat on the floor and picked up the most detailed drawings. Closing her eyes, she touched the paper and became immediately transformed into the art. Upon opening her eyes, she found herself in the black and white, roughly rendered scene. Even on paper, the still serenity of the final resting place for so many settled around her. Bella walked among the rows, kneeling to investigate the once painted lines in relation to the rest of the structures.

"Anything?" Markus asked his quiet voice in the air around her.

She wished surfaces could be conveyed in art, but she could only examine visuals in more depth with her talent. "The texture is odd like it's risen. Thick. I've never seen paint like this."

"What is going on? What's happening?" Leander's voice floated around, and Bella smiled.

"Her talent," Markus said, and nothing more. "Anything else, Bella?"

She explored the space, her fingers sliding to the next image to examine a crypt in more detail or an isolated line as though she were on the ground with the magnifying glass. Despite being unable to explore the surface, learn if it was rough or smooth, or thick enough to form a ridge on the ground it'd been painted on, she still reached out and ran her fingers along the border.

Standing within the image, she shifted her hand in her corporeal form and appeared in front of an old family crypt. Lines and lines of what she figured were names and dates were etched into brick faces. Tattered remnants of fabric hung from loops at the top of each vault. Geometric shapes were shaded onto the edges, making her wonder if they were painted art and as bright as the rest of the culture she'd experienced.

Slowly, she extracted herself from the scenes, the cemetery floor fading from her mind. "I'd like to see one of the cemeteries for this city."

"Now?" Leander asked, adjusting his lenses over wide eyes.

Bella glanced out the window. "There should be enough light, yes?"

Leander scratched behind his ear and shifted his shoulders. "What do you think there's to find at a cemetery?"

"I want to compare the past to the present," Bella said. "Retrace Oberon's thoughts. Besides, the view from those buildings is high enough, maybe we'll see something."

"Won't hurt," Markus agreed. He turned his attention to Leander. "We'll bring the journals, and you bring the letters he sent. Maybe from the vantage point, we can narrow down where his interest was and try to find evidence of the site."

Leander perked up at that. He set the journal on the stack with the others. "I will meet you downstairs with them."

Bella gathered the drawings together, tapping them on the floor to align them before rising. "Do you think it's a good idea? To go?"

Markus took the papers from her and set them next to the journals. "I think you want to go, even without the case, so we will go."

"I do want to," she admitted. "But I also want

to see what Oberon did. How he came to his conclusion."

"You've already seen what he did. You already made the connection."

Bella propped her hands on her hips and stared out the window again. The vertical cemetery was a speck on the horizon beyond the city. "Maybe we should just study the journals and letters and figure out where he went from here."

Markus took her hands and drew her close. The scent and nearness of him grounded and enticed. "You want to start where he started, and so we will. No argument."

Forcing away her insecurities, she nodded. "All right. Let's go."

CHAPTER

EIGHT

A DRY, WESTERN WIND WHIPPED THROUGH THE corridors of the vertical cemetery. Bella grasped the waist-high wall and viewed the desert. Miles and miles of sand, shrubbery, skinny trees, and massive boulders dotted the landscape. The clouds were beginning to glow with a faint creamy pink against an indigo sky. The colors were promising to be spectacular. Bella braced her arms and settled her weight on the rough brick, enjoying the solitude only a cemetery seemed capable of providing.

Lunah sat beside her, the wolf's height allowing her to see the view. Whining, she yawned, her long tongue curling and then flopping free. Bella patted between her ears. Somewhere on one of the many levels, Leander and Markus examined the letters and journals, trying to find any landmarks Oberon may have mentioned from the vantage point.

Bella pushed away from the barrier and wandered along the corridors created by tombs. Long streamers of fabric fluttered and danced in the breeze. The family colors were tied around large metal hoops at the top of each burial site. The unity of marriage was evident by the dozens of colors most tombs displayed. Some vaults had painted borders. Others had been mosaicked or etched. A few were a combination of decorations. They all had personal touches that made them unique.

A part of Bella wished there had been such a personal way to say goodbye to her father. But the frigid temperatures for months of the year and feet of snow, ice, and permafrost grounds made anything more than stone monuments placed where the family wished, either burying ashes or scattering them impossible. Indoor mausoleums were few, and only the wealthy used them. They had placed a stone in a community lot for her father and his ashes and visited it annually. Well, Bella did. Her siblings had long stopped the tradition, which they'd only honored at Madeleine's request. Once their mother had stopped inviting their presence, they'd quit attending.

Bella stopped at a full row, scuffing her toe along the gritty stone floor. Whole slabs of quarried stone were fitted together to create the illusion of a solid surface, much like the parking decks they were designed after. The engineering needed to lay each floor was a remarkable testament to mankind's ingenuity, even after the fall of technological advances. Bella crouched down and brushed away built-up sand along the bottom edge of each tomb, checking again to ensure she didn't miss the painted lines. Traditions were a funny thing. They didn't just stop happening. If the original builders had used lines, the ones today would, too. But if they hadn't... the lines wouldn't have transferred as a design element to a new location.

Oberon's theory was proving correct.

Lunah's claws scrambling on the stone floor had Bella rising. She moved toward the nearest set of stairs and looked over the rail. Markus glanced up, smiling, the golden light catching in his eyes. Bella's heart thumped hard in her chest. How had *this* man chosen her? The tattoo on her back seemed to tingle, sending an echoing shiver through her body, awakening every nerve. An answering heat ignited in his gaze. She returned his smile.

"Did you find anything?" she asked, leaning over the rail for her voice to carry.

Lunah waited at the top of the steps, tail swinging in a quick, wide arc. Markus grabbed her muzzle when he could reach, playfully shaking her head before urging her to step back so he could access the landing. "We think we did."

Bella straightened. "Fantastic."

"*Dak*, let me show you." He held a hand toward the right.

Bella stepped into his side, and he dropped his hand to her hip. "Where's Leander?"

"Down two levels. He saw some decorated tombs he wanted to investigate further. He said the historian in him was desperate for a closer look."

Bella could understand, and she wasn't a historian. He led her to the other side of the floor. Wind tossed her curls around and molded her shirt to her torso. Markus gave a masculine groan of approval, causing her cheeks to flush. Unwelcome and unbidden, the thought of what his other lovers were like in their figure intruded on her joy. Were they curvier? Prettier? Did he prefer aspects of them to what he was stuck with now?

He stopped near the corner, where a wider view of the desert spread out before them. Wrapping his arms around her waist, he pulled her tight against his chest and rested his chin on her shoulder. "What are you worried about, mate?"

"I just want to find out what's happened to Oberon," she said, ignoring the unease at lying. Or at least altering her truth.

"Mmm," he hummed into her ear, nuzzling her neck. "We will."

"What do you have to show me?"

"Dangerous question to ask when we're here alone," he whispered, pressing his front to her back, where his desire was unmistakable.

He kissed the jumping pulse in her neck, causing her breath to catch. Bella wrapped her hands around his wrists and held tight, her nails pressing into the leather of his bracers. What had she been lamenting? Oh yes... that perhaps he didn't—one of his hands moved to cup her breast, while the other ventured further south—want her. How very—oh summer sun, his skilled fingers teased the sensitive flesh above the waist of her pants—foolish of her. His touch was gentle, fleeting, building a desire she desperately wanted him to finish.

"I just needed to feel you, *krahet'sna*."

Beautiful. As if he knew she needed to hear how he felt about her. How he saw her. Bella allowed her weight to settle fully against him, her head falling back onto his shoulder. Perhaps he did. And she could find no room to be embarrassed by her insecurity. Not now, with his delicate touch reminding her of the pleasure he could deliver. But this was not the place, and now was not the time to indulge in such carnality.

"Markus." She drew his name out on a long exhale as a shiver of pleasure raced from her core.

"Mmm?" He licked her neck, and her inner muscles clenched.

"What did you and Leander find?" she somehow managed to articulate.

Slowly, he extracted his hand from under her clothes and stopped the gentle tracing of her nipple. He kissed her cheek and sighed. "You are right, I need to stop."

"I wish you didn't," she said before she could stop herself.

"Being quiet has benefits, but I like the sound of your pleasure too much to hold anything back." He kissed her cheek again and stepped away. The loss of his body heat and presence was immediate, and Bella reached for him. He pulled her into his side but kept his hold loose. "Do you see the cluster of large boulders off to the right?"

Bella narrowed her gaze on the area he pointed out and nodded. "Yes."

"Oberon mentions them in his journal. On the other side of them, he found some unearthed cement pillars after an aggressive wind storm. The storms are known for uncovering many long-buried secrets all over this continent."

"How long of a walk do you think it is? Could we even walk it?" she wondered.

"Probably a couple of hours, and Oberon made the journey, so I think we'll be fine. Lunah will scout ahead for us."

Knowing Lunah would ensure their safety relieved Bella. She knew nothing about the dangers lurking beyond civilization, though she'd read plenty about the wildlife alone to make her nervous. Venomous snakes and lizards. Aggressive predatory birds. Large feral cat and dog species. She had no idea if they were a danger to the local population or if, like many species in the inhabited world, the dangerous ones tended to thrive in the uninhabited zones.

"We'll get up in the morning, around sunrise, and try to leave before anyone could think to follow us," he said.

Bella glanced up at him, frowning. "Do you think we're being watched?"

"To a point, *dak*. Lunah has caught the same scent on the wind three times now."

"They followed us here?"

"To here, but not once it was clear where we were going. Tomorrow, as we pass this structure, might prove different." He shifted forward, his arm dropping from around her waist to brace on the half-wall. The silver rings on his fingers flashed in the weakening light of day as he threaded their hands together. "Part of me hopes they do follow, then we'll know we're on the right path, and perhaps they'll reveal themselves. Someone is curious about our investigation, and I'd like to know why."

Tepid water rained down on Bella. The chilly drops slid down her skin, but her shiver wasn't from the cold. On his knees before her, the wet length of his hair plastered to his back, Markus gripped her thigh slung over his shoulder in one hand. Breathless from the pleasure rippling from her center, Bella glanced down at the same moment her very skilled husband leaned back to look up at her. His other fist worked his erection, adding to Bella's excitement.

In less than twenty-four hours, he'd taught her so much about herself, and she knew they had so much more to discover. Good and bad. She wasn't a fool. She knew there'd be compromises and outright refusals on both their parts. His mouth on her was not one of those moments. She'd wanted to do the same to him, but he wasn't ready. No one had given him pleasure before outside of basic sex, something she'd been more than delighted to learn. There'd be something exclusive between them, and she couldn't wait to discover what he loved, like her. Markus feared she'd dislike doing anything more than accepting him into her body. Bella disagreed, but she'd fight the battle to prove as much to him.

Only a single lantern provided a soft glow for the bathroom. The sun had yet to rise. They'd awakened with the intent of getting ready and meeting Leander downstairs, but the moment

Bella had shed her clothes and stepped into the shower, Markus had thrown their intentions out the window. She didn't care. The sensations he made her feel were too addictive for her thoughts to stray farther than the next second when she'd be immersed in sensuality.

He kissed the hollow of her hip. Licked an erotic trail to the center of her belly, where he rose higher on his knees, dislodging her leg, and took one of her nipples into his mouth. Bella speared her fingers into his hair, weighed down by the water. If it were up to her, he'd never braid the length again. She liked it free, framing his handsome face, flowing down his back and shoulders. But he'd said such was only ever for her to see, and she couldn't argue with the intimacy of knowing she alone knew how he looked relaxed. Unguarded.

Rising, his large frame blocked the spray of cool water. She reached for the hard length, jutting proudly from his body, but he caught her hand and squeezed. Frustrated, she tried to yank her hand free.

"I want to feel you," she whispered.

"Not yet," he breathed, "I'll come all over you if you touch me."

"Good," she growled. "Why would that be bad?"

"There's nothing for you."

Bella tried to reach with her other hand, but he caught her wrist and pinned both above her to the cold tile. "The experience would be for me. Let me have it, Markus."

The inner battle played across his features,

tightening his muscles. His gaze searched hers, and she arched her torso and tugged at her wrists.

"Please."

For tense seconds, his eyes searched hers as if looking for some shred of doubt or aversion to exploring him in the same manner he'd explored her. Or at least what he'd allow. Bella tried her hardest to convey her need to feel him, to watch the moment he experienced an orgasm.

One finger at a time, he released his hold on her wrists. Bella's heart leaped, and anticipation flushed across her skin. Shaking, she wrapped her hand around his thick shaft, gasping at the solid heft of him. A pulse tapped against her palm. Grunting, he tilted his head back. Water flowed over his shoulders, down his stomach, and splashed against her fingers, gripping him.

"What do I do?" she asked.

Markus reached over to the stall shelves set into the corner where little bottles of soaps in various scents were placed for their use. After opening one, he poured the slick contents over himself and her hand. "What feels right."

A spiced citrus scent filled the space between them, and Bella tested the difference, smiling when her hand slid easily along his flesh. The accompanying groan from him and the faintest zing of enjoyment along their bond emboldened her. He felt amazing, like steel wrapped in flesh. Testing where her touch affected him the most, she discovered his hips jerked when she reached the tip, and he'd visibly tighten. At one point, he braced an arm over her shoulder, his head hanging, hair molded to his chest, muscles clenched in harsh relief. He was a sight she couldn't take her eyes from. She soon found a rhythm, stroking, watching bubbles glide along the darker tone of his skin.

She knew the exact moment he quit fighting the experience and let go. He grabbed her hip hard, and his erratic breaths rushed past her ear. His hips moved in time to her motions, a rolling that she swore she could feel deep inside despite only her hand touching him.

Excitement and desire made her squirm, but he didn't allow her to ride out the storm alone. The sudden pressure of his fingers on her clit made her jump. He didn't ease her into the experience. Oh no, they were far past gentle, and she was beyond ready for him. One finger thrust into her, pulled out and was replaced by a second. Bella cried out, her eyes squeezing shut at the pleasure.

"Come for me," he growled.

Bella's fingers tightened around him, and with a hard shudder, his hot seed marked her stomach. The subtle pulsing beneath her palm and the evidence of his release triggered her own, and she widened her stance to take his fingers deeper, prolonging her climax.

The tranquil drumming of water on the tile eased Bella back into reality. Slowly, she removed her hand from him and became aware of him easing from her body. He rested his forehead on hers, his heavy breaths brushing her lips.

"Well?" Bella couldn't help but ask, touching

a curious hand to the glistening mess on her belly.

"Well, what?" he asked.

"Will we be able to do that again? Or more?"

He straightened and blinked down at her. "More?"

She wrapped her arms around his shoulders and stood on her tiptoes to whisper into his ear, "There's still one more part of me that wants to know what you'll feel like."

"*Dsi vefi cna moarta'sie,*" he ground out, the hand still on her hip clenching.

"What does that mean?" she asked, whispering.

"You are going to kill me."

She pushed him into the water, letting the spray rinse them both before jumping him. She trusted him to catch her, and he did, his arms banding around her back and under her rear. His shoulders slammed into the tile wall behind him. Before kissing him, she tossed wet hair from her face. Her fingers pressed into the firm muscles of his shoulders as her mouth opened for his tongue. All the passion from their shared pleasure exploded between them in their kiss.

Breathless, she pulled back. "I'm not done with you yet, so no dying allowed."

He groaned and retook her mouth.

The sun was glowing along the horizon when they finally emerged, pruned from too much water and loose-jointed from their sensual indulgence. Bella wanted to flop onto the bed and take a nap. Markus followed her thoughts and grasped her arm, spinning her around toward her bag.

"After the search, we'll go back to bed," he said.

"Will we sleep this time?" she asked, yawning, enjoying all the delicious little tingles and twinges that were a testament to time well spent.

"I have no idea, will we?"

Bella looked over his nude form and bit her lip. She shrugged.

He laughed, stroked her bottom, and pointed at the bag. "Clothes. Now."

Bella picked up her bag and dug inside until she found something comfortable for a long walk in the sand. A loose pair of navy linen pants, a peach silk tunic, and a pair of brown leather sandals. She pulled on appropriate undergarments before donning the rest. Markus was affixing a leather bracer to his left wrist when a knock rattled their door.

"It's open," Markus called.

Bella raised her brows. "You left the door unlocked?"

"No, I let Lunah out while you were looking for clothes."

Leander walked in, and Bella had to cut off a bark of laughter. A huge hat flopped over his head. The entirety of his nose was painted white, along with his chin. Two dark gray lines were drawn underneath the frames of his glasses on his cheeks. The collar of his white shirt was pulled up to underneath his chin.

He pointed at his cheeks. "Keeps the sun from glaring into my eyes." He dug around into his pants pocket and produced a folded compact. "Care for some?"

Quirking a brow, Markus took the small metal case. Glittery beads shimmered in the morning light, revealing a geometric pattern in green, orange, and blue. "Where did you get this?"

"A street vendor on the way home last night. She handed me this when I asked for a way to block the sun." Leander pointed at the ornate compact. "She said it was perfect."

Markus opened the compact. Bella leaned over and looked at the shades of rich gray, white, and silver. A mirror was set into the top.

"Close your eyes," Markus whispered.

Bella obeyed. His gentle touch skimmed her eyelids, dabbed at the crease, and brushed along the corners. Bella's eyes fluttered open when the case clicked shut.

"I think the vendor meant *for* eyes," Markus said, returning the makeup. "Not to block the sun from them."

"Oooh," Leander breathed, adjusting his glasses. "My. Yes, perhaps. Though I think it'll work for my purposes, too?"

Markus smiled, his knuckles caressing under Bella's jaw. "I'm sure."

Curious, Bella went to the bathroom to see her reflection. A smoky-eyed woman with startling blue-green eyes stared back at her. Her curls, a wild drying mess around her head, looked exotic instead of frizzy. Bella blinked, turning her face left and then right. Her jaw dropped. Markus appeared behind her, wrapping his arm around her upper chest and kissed her temple.

"Beautiful," he whispered and pressed another kiss to her temple.

"What did you do?" She continued to inspect her face.

"Just applied a small amount of eyeshadow. My cousin doesn't go anywhere without some on."

"The artist cousin?" Bella asked, lifting her chin. How could something so small make such a difference?

"Yes. Do you like?"

"I'm not sure yet."

He released her. "If you like it or don't is up to you."

She continued to stare at herself. "Do *you* like it?"

"You are stunning regardless. This draws attention to aspects of your unique beauty."

Warmth bloomed across her cheeks. She'd never considered herself any great beauty, but when Markus looked at her.... She sighed in happiness. He kissed her temple and left her alone, staring at her reflection.

Enough with the distractions, they'd wasted the morning already. And no, she wasn't complaining, but they couldn't afford any further interruptions. Bella pulled her hair into a twist and secured it atop her head with a clip as she joined the two men in the sitting area. "Ready."

Markus hefted a pack over his shoulder and motioned for Leander to lead the way from their room. "Do you have the journal with the landmark entry?"

"Yes," Leander said, patting the pockets of his lumpy vest. "I also brought his last letter where he describes the section he found, so we can match it if we find it."

At the bottom of the stairs, they found a packed bag with bottles of juice and wrapped food packages. Bella placed the bag into Markus's pack. "A'ki is doing far more for us than he's earning for our stay."

"This is their way," Leander said. "We repay him by speaking kindly of his establishment and honoring his hospitality."

Lunah was waiting for them at the end of the walkway to the street. Markus ruffled between her ears, and after touching her nose to Bella's palm, she took off with a happy spring to her steps.

"Will she tell you if she catches the scent of the person following us yesterday?" Bella asked once Leander was a few steps in front.

"Yes. I'm hoping it's too early for our shadow."

Peach and lavender clouds streaked a soft gray sky. The pale orb of the sun crested over the top of the mountains as they walked past the last occupied house in the city. A brightly clothed teenage girl snapped a dusty rug from a front window, waved, and returned to her task. Bella took a deep breath of clean, cool morning air. A dog barked in the distance. The only other disturbance to the quiet was the crunch of their shoes in the sand and grit. They walked in silence, each lost in thought, following an invisible trail left for them by a missing man.

The towering vertical cemetery cast a long shadow as they passed by. Bella shielded her eyes from the rising sun and looked up. Long fabric streamers blew from the tombs closest to the edge, fluttering like memorial banners. A stooped old man carried a basket laden with fabric up the winding stairs. Bella stopped for a moment to observe the solitary trek, wondering whose ribbons he was replacing with fresh material.

Markus brushed her elbow, smiled, and followed her attention to the man disappearing on the sixth floor. Only once he was no longer visible could Bella bring herself to move. She laced her fingers through Markus's, needing the contact.

Up ahead, Leander followed behind Lunah, looking up from the journal to stay on the path the wolf set and then back to the book. The hat flopped on his head, casting an odd silhouette over his shadow on the ground. Light glared off the white paint on his nose and chin. A steady breeze blew his long-sleeve shirt tight across his thin chest and arms and ruffled the held pages of the journal.

In contrast, Markus strode with his sleeves rolled up, his braid swinging along his back, the bright sun soaking into his rich caramel skin. His gaze continually searched the surrounding desert. The heavy shadow of his beard accented his jaw and cheeks. Bella's heart did a little turn in her chest. She knew intimately how his facial hair's rough yet silky texture felt against her skin.

How that powerful body felt over her. Within her.

The sun slid a lazy path over the sky as they hiked. Markus stopped three hours into their journey and handed out bottled juice and food. Lunah wandered off to drink from a puddle and rest in the shade of a boulder.

Leander fiddled with his hat and brushed sand from his lower pant legs. Squinting at the sky, he scrunched his nose and looked around. "We must be getting close."

"Let me see the journal." Markus motioned with his fingers.

Bella refreshed herself while the two men looked over the notes from the journal and the letter. Sandwich in hand, Markus climbed onto the tallest boulder. He ate from his perch, and Bella was content to sit back and take in all the views, her husband among them. Lunah meandered over and flopped down at Bella's feet. Bella rubbed the toe of her shoe along the wolf's belly.

Markus hopped down from the boulder, landing in a perfect crouch at the base. Lunah jumped up, every muscle coiled. Man and beast looked at each other. Power thrummed along their bond, an odd surge that had Bella wanting to leap to attention, too.

"What is it?" Bella asked.

Lunah bolted, sand spraying behind her. Markus slowly stood. "I saw the cement columns. I want to make sure no one is hiding."

Bella stood. "Did she scent our shadow?"

"No, but that doesn't mean they aren't waiting for us."

Leander moved to stand beside Bella. He crumpled his food wrapper between his palms. "Are we close after all?"

"I believe so," Bella said, taking the waxed paper from him and joining it to her own. She went to Markus's pack and placed the empty bottles and other refuse from their lunch into an outside pocket. "Lunah is making sure it's safe."

Markus shouldered the bag. "Come on, this way. Lunah doesn't scent anything that shouldn't be there."

Anticipation hummed through Bella. If this was the site of Oberon's discovery, they might be within walking distance of answers. She wanted to rush past Markus and see what he'd seen from his rock perch.

The first pillar came into view as they rounded a boulder. A stubby, crumbling square with rusted metal poking upward from the sand. Lunah sniffed around a similar, taller half-rectangle that looked to have once been a doorway or perhaps the upper level of something. Maybe a window? The crumbling ruins were ambiguous, with no reference but sand, shrubs, boulders, and mountains off in the distance. Chunks of cement, large hunks of rusted metal, and glittering glass mixed amongst the sand and rocks between massive boulders. Leander touched everything with reverence, his eyes wide behind his frames.

"This is it," Leander said, spinning around to encounter another decaying cement beam lying where it'd fallen centuries ago. "This is what Oberon found."

"It's what led him to a larger discovery,"

Markus corrected, hands on his hips as he glanced around. "Where's the entrance to his cave?"

Bella shielded her eyes from the sun's harsh glare and wandered between two large stones that seemed to have merged with concrete posts. An ominous crack was her only warning before the ground disappeared beneath her. Sand rained down in the darkness. Her butt landed on something hard, jarring her tailbone and sending pain shooting up her spine. Spinning in the dark, she reached out for anything, fear stealing her breath. Her left side connected with another hard object, but instead of falling into a continuing void, she slid along a gritty surface into the unknown. A scream tore free as she picked up speed, her forearm scraping along the rough plane.

Bella! My Bella! Lunah's frantic cry sounded in her mind. No pain accompanied the intrusion this time. Or perhaps too many other places hurt within her to notice.

Her slide came to an end on a softer surface. Rolling in sand, Bella came to stop face first, coughing and spitting grit from her mouth. Her first attempt to rise failed as her left arm and hip refused to hold her weight. Taking a second to catch her breath, she tried again. Thick sand displaced beneath her palms.

Something falling echoed in the dark void surrounding her. Fear pierced through her, and she pulled her knees into her chest, blinking, trying her hardest to make out anything. Another echo accompanied scratching, followed by a yip.

"Lunah?" Bella stood, wobbling on trembling legs, reaching out in the darkness for something to steady herself and encounter nothing but endless space.

Here, my Bella, I'm here, the wolf said.

A wet nose pressed into Bella's outstretched palm. Tears burned her eyes. Falling to her knees, she wrapped the wolf in a tight hug. "Oh, Lunah. Why? Now we're both trapped down here."

Markus is coming for us, Markus is.

Debris rained down from above, and a crack of light appeared. The opening grew until Bella could begin to make out shadows in the darkness around her. With the new sensory input, her other senses began to awaken beyond the haze of her panic. Somewhere deep within the void, the faint rush of water mingled with sharper echoes of rubble cascading from overhead. Mildew tainted the stagnant air and something far more unpleasant.

Death.

The sulfuric stench of decay slowly permeated the space around Bella until it was all she could do not to choke and gag. More light filtered in from above. Bella didn't want to look around. Didn't want to see what she'd fallen into.

Oberon Rima's grave.

CHAPTER

NINE

Markus yanked at another board, popping inadequately hammered nails free with ease. He held the plank in Leander's direction. "Keep wiping sand away. They need to all be gone, or we'll never be able to see our way down."

He tossed the board and went on to the next, careful to keep his knees on the hopefully solid ground beneath him. Leander nodded and continued to use his hat to displace sand, exposing the hastily built camouflage over the fissure Bella had tumbled down.

There is a body, there is, Lunah conveyed to him along their bond.

Markus paused, squeezing his eyes shut and hanging his head. *Thank you, Lunah. Bella is okay?* he asked again, needing to know his mate was indeed all right. He couldn't sense much now, unsure if she was safe or unconscious or what may be happening. When she'd fallen, her terror had sent him to his knees. Knowing he was helpless in the situation had kept him there.

She is bleeding, she is.

Anxiety gripped him, and he had to fight the urge to leap down the hole before he'd finished giving them the safest option possible by seeing their route. He'd be no good to her, injured or dead, because he'd rushed getting to her. But to assure himself, he sank deeper into his bond with Lunah until he could experience the dark depths they were trapped within. Little could be seen, but vague outlines of structures stretched in every direction. Bella sat in the sand, her skin pale and dusted with grit. She grasped Lunah's jaw, her gaze meeting Lunah's and, therefore, *his*, her lips moving. The urge to open another sense and hear her beautiful voice had his jaw clenching.

She says to tell you she is fine, to be careful, she says.

I will be. Do not move from where you are. Markus withdrew, satisfied they were as safe as they could be.

"Can you tell where it ends?" Markus asked Leander, throwing another chunk of wood away.

Leander crawled in the sand, brushing his fingers through the coarse soil. "I think... yes, here, right here." He yanked on a board, and the remaining construction slid and then teetered into the opening.

Watch out below! Markus warned Lunah. He lay on his stomach and tried to see into the void, but only blackness yawned at him.

"Oh no, I'm so sorry," Leander said, joining him on his belly to peer below. "My, that is quite dark. How will we get down there?"

"There is a way. Oberon found it and used it more than once."

Markus stood, dusted himself off, and slowly walked around the hole. Oberon's venturing would have left evidence. A worn spot on the edge caught his attention, and Markus knelt, touching the crumbling indent along the decaying cement. Spinning on his heel, he searched the ground, smiling when he caught the coiled length of rope hidden between two rocks. He tugged, finding where it'd been attached. A methodical check ensured the anchor was secure and the rope was in good enough condition to use.

Hefting the length over his forearm, Markus peered over the edge, spotting the first foothold Oberon must have used to begin the climb down. "I suggest you head back to town, Mr. Kavont. The route is safe."

Leander lifted his chin, squared his shoulders, and adjusted the ridiculous oversized hat on his head. "I would prefer to come with you."

Markus peered down into the black crevice. "I can't guarantee your safety."

"This is not my first time in the field. I'm aware of the risks."

Markus hesitated, took a deep breath, and met the resolute dark eyes behind the glasses. "There is a body. Chances are high it's Oberon."

Leander recoiled, blinking in disbelief. He pressed a hand to his chest and half-turned away. "You are um... that is, perhaps you are..." He cleared his throat, shaking his head. "I'm sorry, it's just how could you possibly know?"

Markus regretted Leander's hurt but saw no use in glossing over the sad truth. "Lunah told me of the remains. Considering someone boarded up the evidence of Oberon's discovery and the death, I assume it's him we will find below. He and whoever did all this," he said, motioning to the wood scraps, "were the only ones who knew of this location."

Leander braced his hands on his hips, sucked in a hard breath through his nose, and nodded, eyes and lips squeezed shut.

Markus clapped a hand on the academic's thin shoulder. "There is no shame in returning to Logasin City. Death is never easy to witness, let alone when it's someone important."

"No." Leander took another deep breath, sniffling. "No, I am a better friend than that. Strangers should not be the only ones to attest to the atrocity committed against him. I've come this far. I'll see it through."

"That is admirable of you. Strangers are often the only witnesses to violent crime."

"You think—" Leander shook his head again, lifted his hand, and squeezed his temples between his thumb and forefinger. "Of course, his death was violent."

Markus patted Leander's shoulder before gripping the rope. "Are you ready?"

"Yes."

"Follow after me. Step where I step. If I say stop, you stop, no questions."

He pulled off his hat and clutched it between both hands. "Should I leave this up here or...?"

"You can leave it wherever you like. If

someone comes by, they'll know we've discovered the site. No hiding that fact now."

Leander glanced around at all the discarded boards. "No, I suppose not."

Markus gathered broken boards that would fit into his pack. They'd need a means of light below. He figured Oberon had likely left a few lanterns, but light would be required to find them. Once his bag was secure, he leaped down the opening to the first ledge, a cracked chunk of cement wedged between two concrete pillars that had fallen to support each other. Time had fused the entire structure together, and now that it was exposed, he figured time would erode them apart again at some point.

"Use the rope as your guide," Markus said, releasing enough line for freedom of movement but keeping it tight enough to help him maintain his balance as he moved from one ledge to another.

Rusted metal cords jutted from every angle, some twisted and gnarled, others straight and dangerously slanted. One wrong move, and either of them would be impaled. He'd never know how Bella had tumbled down with little more than bruises and some scuffs. At least, he hoped that's all she'd suffered from the fall. The light filtering in from above was enough until around halfway down, where the shadows became longer, making it harder to judge distances, and the downward trek slowed. Markus could make out the end, however, his eyes adjusting to the dimness enough to see hints of the sandy floor. He also spotted faint movement and waved.

Lunah's bark echoed upward. Sand and pebbles rained down as Leander slipped. Markus waited, glancing over his shoulder to ensure the academic wasn't in any distress. Leander raised a hand, and his other gripped the rope with white knuckles.

"I'm going to move faster," Markus said. "Will you be all right on your own from here?"

Leander looked up and then around. "Yes, I made it this far. I'll be fine."

Markus's need to get to his wife and wolf overrode his concern for the inexperienced historian. He'd do his best to anchor the rope in safe places, ensuring Leander could steady himself and continue at his own pace. A sluggish speed Markus could no longer tolerate. Utilizing his enhanced reflexes and senses, thanks to his beast master genetic trait, Markus swiftly navigated the remaining ruins. An unpleasant whiff of death floated around him, and he scrunched his nose. Hopefully, he wouldn't land on top of the body. The final stretch was a seven-foot drop, which he leaped with ease, leaving the rope to dangle over the edge for when Leander finally arrived.

Sand puffed around him and cushioned his feet when he landed. He struggled to take a stable step, falling to a knee on the soft, unsteady ground. Bella was in a similar predicament, fighting against the yielding soil in an effort to reach him. Tears ran muddy tracks down her cheeks and dripped from her jaw. Markus worried she was injured more than he could see. The fabric of her shirt was torn on both her arms, but blood only stained her left sleeve.

They collided in a fierce hug. Markus held her to his chest, one hand cupping the back of her head, the other wrapped around her. She trembled in his arms, and he leaned back, took her face between his palms, and wiped her tears. Lunah bounced around them both, spraying sand in every direction.

"Where are you hurt?" he asked.

She grasped his biceps. "I'm fine, really. Just thankful you made it down safely to me."

After pressing a quick kiss to her forehead and then her lips, not caring about the grit, he took hold of her injured arm and slid the sleeve to try to see the extent of the damage. The meager light from the opening above didn't give him much more than a vague impression of her raw flesh. Lunah still danced around, and Markus signaled for her to calm. She dropped to her stomach and gave a quiet *woof*.

Frustrated, he released Bella's arm and grabbed for his pack. He removed the wood fragments he'd packed, throwing them on the ground before digging around inside for a box of matches. Using his foot to toss up one of the boards, he snatched it from the air and stabbed it into the ground. A burst of sulfur filled the air a second before the match flared to life. He touched the flame to the end of the dry chunk of wood. The fire soon spread to cover the top, giving them some much-needed light. Bella let out a long exhale, looking around. Markus didn't care about the sights. He grasped her arm again, angling the wound toward the glow. Little chunks of rock and grains of blood-soaked sand dotted the injury, covering the underside of her forearm from elbow to wrist. She hissed and tried to free her arm when he dislodged one of the pebbles from her skin.

He gently wrapped his fingers around her hand. "I am sorry, *krahet'sna*. I must clean this."

"I know." She squeezed her eyes closed. "I'm sorry, it just hurts."

Markus's heart clenched, and he kissed the inside bend of her arm. "I know. I'll try to be fast."

"I wish we knew where the water was," she murmured, angling her arm to see better.

Markus tilted his head and listened to the distant rush of water. "In this cavernous space, it could be too far for us to reach."

"Or down another hole."

"That too." He dropped to a crouch and dug around in his pack. He pulled out a jar of water and a clean rag. "This will have to do."

He saturated the cloth with water and gently rubbed the grit and easily removable pebbles from her skin. She remained quiet, stiffening when he had to spend extra time on one area. When he finished, he could see where a few rocks were embedded. Sighing, he reached behind his back and removed his knife.

"Hold very still," he commanded, meeting her gaze briefly before focusing on the rocks needing to be dislodged.

A scattering of stones and debris clanked and scuttled behind him, followed quickly by a shout of alarm. Markus dropped the knife to his side, jaw clenched. Bella gasped and then snorted, covering her mouth with her good hand.

"I am afraid to ask," Markus sighed.

She snickered behind her hand. "He's going to need your help."

Markus flipped the knife along his forearm and held out the handle. "Keep this for me."

"Hello?" Leander shouted. "H-hello? Can anyone hear me? Hello? I appear to be quite stuck! Anyone?"

Markus hung his head and sighed again. "I'm coming, Mr. Lavont."

"Oh, thank you. I can't seem to see anything down here. Oh, wait, now I... oh, you're gone again."

Markus turned and found Leander hanging upside down by one leg from the rope, spinning a slow turn underneath an angled chunk of concrete. Markus trudged his way through the sand to stand beneath the wayward historian. Though skewed, the man's glasses were still somehow affixed to his face and covered in dust.

What is wrong with him, what is wrong? Lunah asked, standing beside him, her head angled as she took in the dangling man.

I have no idea, Markus replied, hands on his hips. "What happened?"

"I don't know," Leander said, exasperated. "I was using the rope as a guide, and then I just fell. There must have been a crack or something. Now, can you please get me down? And what is that *awful* stench?"

Markus rubbed his hands down his face. He

feared if he answered Leander's question, the man was liable to vomit all over himself, and, due to proximity, Markus. No, thank you. He slogged back to the stack of discarded wood, grabbed a slat and his matches, and returned to Leander. Hopefully, poor Oberon wasn't lying within visual distance of where Leander dangled, but it was a risk Markus had to take. He couldn't get the man down without light. He set the board into the sand, lit it on fire, and reviewed the situation.

The rope had knotted several times around Leander's ankle and calf. If Markus didn't get him down soon, the length would begin to not only cut off vital circulation but into flesh. He needed more rope and a way to anchor to get above the problem.

Can you scent Oberon? Is there a familiar trail from what you learned of him at his apartment? Markus asked Lunah.

Not over the scent of his death, not over.

Can you please try? I need to find his base of operations down here. He'd have left supplies there.

She yipped and took off into the darkness.

"What is going on? Can't you cut me down?" Leander asked, doing another slow rotation.

Markus looked up. "She's going to search for Oberon's camp. I need rope to get to you. I can't reach from here to cut you down, and then we'd be trapped if I did."

"My foot is beginning to throb."

Yes, Markus imagined the strangled appendage was beginning to hurt. If Markus didn't find the site, Leander would be in greater trouble than hanging upside down in the dark.

"Don't look to your left," Markus said over his shoulder.

Bella froze, the makeshift torch she carried clutched in her right hand. "W-why?"

"I can see Oberon."

Bella immediately looked at the sandy ground to her right. She'd only seen a decaying dead body through her talent, never in real life. She didn't want to start today, if possible. Thankfully, they'd become somewhat used to the smell. At least it didn't seem much worse. Which was awful. Bella hated everything about the situation. "Can we get to the campsite?"

"Yes, but he's very near it."

"I wonder if he was down here working when he was killed."

"Likely. I'll know more later." He labored ahead, his heavier weight sinking further into the soft sand more than she did with each step. "It appears he managed to get his workstation up onto some sort of foundation."

"Let me know when it's safe to look."

"Once you're up the steps, just don't look behind us."

The first brick step came into view, half buried in sand. Four steps led to a concrete pad, where a canvas awning had been erected over tables set into a horseshoe along the edges. A table in the center held all sorts of broken bits of objects, some Bella had never seen and wouldn't even begin to guess what they might be. Crates were lined beneath the tables. Markus lit a lamp hanging from the center of the canopy and then went back down the steps with his torch. He stuck the torch into the sand, ember side down, and Bella did the same. He kicked sand over both the smoldering wood fragments.

"We need to find rope. We'll inventory the other supplies after I get Leander down."

"How's he doing?" Bella pulled out the first crate and found hay and canvas-wrapped packages. She shoved it back and went to the next one.

"Lunah says his whining has increased."

"Poor guy." Two more crates proved useless. "I'm sure his thoughts of adventures didn't include hanging upside down with his foot in jeopardy of being amputated."

"Just as yours didn't include falling." Markus opened a chest. "Found some." He yanked out a length and an odd claw-shaped apparatus. "Will you be okay here by yourself?"

"Yes. I'll see if I can find a better first aid kit." The rocks still in her forearm stung, but Leander's emergency came first.

"I'll send Lunah back to you." He dug inside the chest and collected a few more items, shoving them in his pockets.

"Markus." She waited until his golden gaze lifted. "I'll be fine. You may need Lunah's eyes to help you."

The body being so near was making him nervous. A very real reminder of the awfulness one human could inflict on another. That Bella knew, an intuitive knowledge conveyed along their bond, made her push another useless crate underneath the table with her foot and go to her mate. She touched his jaw and caressed down his throat to the small exposed area of skin on his chest, where she pressed her hand. No, he did not want to leave her alone in a dark cavern, with the unknown and a decaying corpse feet away. She rose on her tiptoes and kissed him.

"I'll be fine," she whispered against his mouth. "I promise not to leave the campsite. I won't even go down the stairs."

"How I love you," he growled and kissed her before she could respond to his earth-shattering declaration.

The heat of his emotions raced across their bond. A warmth that suffused every cell in her body. Different from the desire that crackled but no less intense. His tongue probed her mouth, and she didn't hesitate, opening for him, accepting the passion of his kiss in the last place she probably should. She clutched his shoulders and allowed herself to get lost in the sensation of him.

For a fraction of a moment, time was theirs. Death didn't linger in the air. An inept historian didn't need rescuing. They weren't trapped at an unknown depth with an unknown enemy above. He pulled back, gave another sexy growl deep in his throat, pressed a hard kiss to her lips, and then was gone where she refused to look, not wanting to catch even a glimpse of Oberon. Instead, she focused on the physical awareness of his love. A knowledge she felt honored to experience. His private emotions laid open for her.

She pressed her hands over her breast, where her heart hammered. Since the bond had been forged, she realized this wasn't the first time she'd experienced the sensation. Which only made her heart swell even more. But now was *not* the time to be all sappy and overcome by feminine joy.

Returning to her search, she dug through Oberon's workstation for anything useful. She had no doubt they'd be staying the night. Hopefully, they could do something about the archaeologist's remains. Otherwise, Bella doubted anyone would rest. She poked around in crates and baskets set in various spots on the tables. Nothing turned up except excavation tools and artifacts. She went to the center of the space and tapped her foot, looking around. What was she missing? He likely spent at least one night, if not more. He'd have a bed, food stored, and other comfort supplies.

Bella lit another lamp and walked to the steps, angling the light away from the area Markus had said Oberon lay. She leaned around the corner of the tent, holding up the lamp. The lantern wasn't enough to penetrate the heavy darkness. Frowning, she eased back and returned to the rear. Leaning over the tables, she swept the canvas panels to the side. Her curiosity paid off. A narrow opening appeared to lead into another room. Two rope ties hung beside each side of the crevice. Bella secured the panels, wondering why the table had been moved to block the area. Had

Oberon suspected someone was unhappy with his discovery and had hidden his personal space?

Bella took several steps back and surveyed the space. The floor had been swept, so any evidence of moving objects was long gone. But if she had to guess… She set the lamp on the floor and grabbed the table in front of the entrance. The legs screeched as she dragged the furniture to the center next to the other table. She wondered how Oberon had managed to get the items down or if he'd somehow found all the tables. They were all different, and if they were almost a thousand years old, they were in remarkable condition. She shifted the crates to the side and picked up the lantern.

Taking a bracing breath, she squared her shoulders and stepped over the odd threshold, like two support beams had fallen to form a doorway at just the right angle to keep them from crumbling on impact. Cobwebs formed a gauzy curtain above, and every crevice not brushed against on the way to the cozy nook Oberon had made himself at home within.

Bella stopped and held up the lamp. A thick mat with tangled blankets lay to the left. Stacked crates and a thick slab of wood formed a desk against the far wall. Papers littered the surface and had been somehow affixed to the wall above. She stepped closer, angling the light to get a better view. Dozens of detailed drawings and scribbled notes covered every available inch of space around the makeshift workstation. A charcoal sketching set was discarded on the floor, the thin rods scattered and broken to lay where they'd fallen from the leather case. Clothes hung from lines strung at an angle across a corner. Crates held jars of food and various juices, along with empty ones that appeared to have been washed, which meant a nearby viable water source. The thought of fresh, cold water made her lick her parched lips.

To distract herself from the sudden onslaught of thirst, Bella set the lamp on the desk and studied Oberon's work. The sketches showed what the shadows hid, a wonderland of a once thriving, far advanced civilization compared to their own. Metal vehicles of enormous size that could seat dozens all at once. Buildings that once stretched into the sky were now stunted and bound against rock. Waterfalls poured from what had once been windows.

A small pile of colorful pebbles caught her attention. She picked one up, the surface cool and smooth. Holding it up to the light, her eyes widened when the glow of the flame passed right through the cobalt coloring. Incredible.

The echo of masculine voices drifted into the small space. Bella palmed the rock and picked up the lantern. Golden eyes glowing in the darkness made her gasp and jump, bumping the desk. Lunah stepped into the fall of light, her tongue lolling, eyes happy. She did a little bounce and dance. Bella smiled.

"Bella," Markus called. "Did you find any medical supplies?"

"Oh shoot," she whispered, making a face at Lunah. "I bet you knew about this area, didn't you?"

"Bella?"

"Back here!" she answered. She glanced down at the translucent blue pebble and tossed it back with the others. She'd been so wrapped up in all the wonders around her that she'd forgotten what she'd been looking for.

Markus did not have the same issue. He shouldered through the opening that had been fine for her but tight for him, took a quick look around, spotted some random box, reached in, pulled something out, and disappeared the way he'd come. Bella blinked and then followed him.

Leander sat propped against cases near the stairs, his right leg extended as he clutched at his thigh, gaze fixed on an unknown point in the darkness through dusty lenses. Tears tracked down his grimy cheeks. His lips were pursed, scrunching his mustache beneath his flared nostrils. Bella wondered if the tears were from pain or the loss of his friend. Perhaps both. When he spotted her, his quick glance in her direction sent a dust plume from his hair.

"All right, let me see that leg, Mr. Kavont," Markus said, crouching down and placing a lamp on the step near Leander's leg along with whatever he'd collected from Oberon's room. "Then we will handle—"

"Yes. Yes, right," Leander said quickly, swiping his hands across his cheeks.

Markus braced a forearm on his knee and looked at Leander, brows drawn. "Are you certain?"

"Yes, very certain. Thank you." A curt nod sent another plume of dirt into the air.

Bella sat next to him, brushing her hand along the ripped seam of his filthy shirt. She didn't pretend not to know what they were discussing. Or rather, Markus was trying to discuss, but Leander clearly couldn't bear to hear the actual words aloud. How much worse would it be when faced with the complete visual horror of death? "Please reconsider."

"He is..." Leander squeezed his eyes tight behind his glasses. "*Was* my friend. I will help. And, I need to see, to be certain."

Bella met Markus's grim stare. While Bella might not have seen the grisly effects of a murder weeks after the fact in person, she'd seen plenty in crime scene renditions. Having been the assistant to an investigator for the serial crimes unit, the ugliness of late discovery had landed on her desk to be organized and filed. From the bleakness reflected in her husband's gaze, she knew his experience was firsthand. He didn't want the same for the kind historian.

Markus shook his head and set down a canvas bag. He dug around inside, removing a rolled length of fabric. "Your friend will not be anything you'll recognize."

"I understand," Leander whispered, pulling up his pant leg to reveal bruised and chafed shin.

Markus shook his head again. "No, I don't think you do." He palpated around Leander's ankle, gently moving the joint left, then right. "Does this hurt much?"

Leander winced and braced his palms on the floor. "A little."

"I'll wrap it up tight, but you'll have to be

careful." Unrolling the start of the bandage, Markus glanced at Bella. "Can you see if you can find anything for him to use as a crutch or cane, please?"

Bella collected a lantern and, with Lunah following, went down the stairs and in the opposite direction of the remains. A quick scan showed a foot trail, something she'd been hopeful to find. All the drawings and notes meant the archaeologist had done a lot of exploring, but he'd have fanned out a little at a time and maintained a familiar trail to keep from getting lost. Sand drifts played peekaboo with a black surface. A road?

Lunah padded ahead, her nose to the ground, her tail swishing a content arc. Bella held up the lantern in a useless effort to try to see up and out. Darkness saturated everything, an endless void that left her shivering. How had Oberon discovered anything with the handful of lamps he'd brought down?

Opting to keep to the trail he'd set, and Lunah followed, Bella visually scoured the ground for anything that could help an injured man hobble around. They wandered until the scent changed to damp earth and rock. The rush of water intensified. A faint glow ahead made her blink and squint. Lunah disappeared through a fissure, and Bella hastened to catch up, feeling vulnerable with the shadows at her back.

Light and sound increased, and when Bella stepped free, she had to shield her eyes from the glare. Blinking, her eyes slowly adjusted, and she gasped in wonder at the surrounding sight. Glass jewels lined a sparkling blue creek, and the iridescent stones twinkled in a rainbow of colors, sending glittery highlights in every direction. Flowering vines climbed upward, reaching with long tendrils to the light pouring in from various sized holes near the top of the cave ceiling. Stalactites glistened overhead, their slow drips adding to the moist atmosphere. Little ferns clung to the cracked wall surface, and moss covered almost everything, giving a tropical feel to the hidden garden.

The thunder of water had her looking to the left, where a fall gushed from what must have been windows at one point. A rock face cut into the jagged remains of a once proud high-rise, providing a solid platform for the water to flow over. A deep pool caught the stream, churning up mist, soaking plants, rocks, and ancient building debris.

Bella plopped onto her butt, too stunned to remain standing. Lunah bounced through the creek, splashing and snapping at the spray she created. She stopped for a moment to sniff then drink the crystalline liquid.

Good, it is good! Come drink, my Bella, come drink.

Once again, the wolf's voice in her mind brought no discomfort. "Did you tell Markus?"

He knows, he is on his way, yes, he knows.

Movement overhead caught Bella's attention and she shielded her eyes from the streaming beams of sun. Little birds flew in and out of the holes, their small bodies silhouetted. A few dipped low, skimming a flower or the water far enough from the spray to remain dry. They paid no mind to the intrusion of their sanctuary. Leaf-green, with bright yellow chests and blue-tipped wings, they appeared to be spawned from the very environment they inhabited.

What felt like seconds later, Markus's presence registered in a wave of awareness behind her. She didn't move from her spot, staring around in wonder, taking in everything, not wanting to forget a single sight. He didn't speak, simply sat beside her, bracing his arms on his raised knees. Bella leaned over and rested her head on his bicep. Sharing the moment with him felt right. A perfect accompaniment to the beauty surrounding them. A wondrous world has arisen from the broken remains of a civilization they knew nothing about.

"I brought what we need to clean your arm. The water will help," Markus said, his voice barely carrying over the boom of the waterfall. "And you need to drink."

Smiling, she lifted her head and looked at him. Tendrils of hair had come free of his braid, dancing around his face from the wind created by the water. A few had become stuck in his beard and Bella freed them, tucking everything behind his ear. She kept her hand on the base of his neck. The warmth of his skin soaked into her fingers, and the thrill of touching him tingled along her arm. "Will you always take care of me now?"

He brushed a fluttering touch across her lips and jaw, his gaze looking over her before meeting her eyes. "You are the most important part of my life now."

Warmth blossomed through her, settling in

her heart like a tight fist. She grasped his hand and allowed him to pull her up as he stood. On shaky legs, she stumbled across the kaleidoscope-colored ground. The smooth pebbles clattered and shifted beneath her feet.

"Are these gems?" she asked, her hand tightening on his to help her keep her balance as the terrain sloped closer to the water.

Markus leaned down and picked up a handful. He tossed the stones around on his palm. "It's glass."

Bella stopped and took one from his palm. "Glass?" She held it up to the light. "How do you know?"

"There's a beach like this one in Ruthenia. When there's a lot of glass refuse, water smooths the broken edges into stones." He tossed the worn fragments into the water. "Eventually, they'll be grains of sand again."

She rubbed her thumb over a round stone, wondering what the dark blue glass had once been. A bottle? Plate? Maybe a pane of glass from a building? "So much of it. Incredible."

"Discoveries like this often are. Oberon found something special, and he knew it."

Bella held the glass tight in her fist. "And was killed over it."

CHAPTER
TEN

BELLA UNTACKED THE LAST SET OF NOTES FROM THE wall in Oberon's personal space. Somewhere out in the vast darkness, Markus and Leander were handling the archaeologist's remains, giving him the peace and respect he deserved. Bella had been tasked with collecting every scrap of research and any artifacts that would back up the findings in his notes to provide proof of his discovery. Their first-hand account would go far, but having irrefutable evidence would ensure they'd be taken seriously.

Each drawing she added to the collection she inspected to compare it to all the gathered objects in the other room. The glass pebbles, an aluminum can with strange symbols and bright colors, a handful of flat multi-colored cards with raised letters, and black strips on the back that broke when handled too hard were all in another crate. Oberon had kept all those smaller items close. Bella would add to them until the crate was full. She moved one, then the other box onto a center table in the research area.

One at a time, she sifted through thick layers of packed hay and fabric-wrapped treasures, isolating things she felt would help solidify Oberon's theories and support his drawings and possibly the notes she couldn't read. Halfway through her search, the men and Lunah returned, filthy and weary. Even the wolf was covered in grit, apparently having helped with the burial efforts. There would be no vertical cemetery vault for Oberon, and Bella frowned in sadness. The murderer had taken so much from the man. Determined that the discovery of the underground ruins would not be one of the stolen life moments, Bella returned to her search with renewed vigor.

"The sun will set soon," Markus said, brushing a hand along her hip. "Do you want to sleep here or near the water?"

Bella thought of the oppressive darkness that not even a lantern would cut through once they extinguished enough of them to sleep. Perhaps the small openings that allowed sun would also allow some moonlight.

Markus smiled, his fingers trailing up her spine. "The water it is."

She inspected another object, trying to decide its importance. A thin metal and glass, something with substantial weight. Odd circles of glass were on the back in the upper left corner, disrupting the smooth surface. Shrugging, she set it in the box. Oberon had a sizeable collection of them, enough to have perhaps mentioned the artifacts in his notes. Maybe he even had an idea of what they'd once been to the people who'd in-habited the site.

"What did you find out about his death?" Bella asked quietly, glancing over her shoulder. Leander sat, shoulders hunched, head in his hands.

"He'd been hit on the head and stabbed. Dozens of times," Markus whispered. "There was dried blood spray everywhere."

"Defensive signs?" she asked, tucking a layer of fabric over the treasures.

Markus shook his head.

Bella's frown deepened. "Then the blow must have knocked him out."

"Yes, and his attacker took out their rage on him."

"At least if he was unconscious, he didn't suffer through his murder."

Markus handed her a layer of hay from an-other crate. "That's what I told Leander. Not that it helped much."

Bella packed in the filler, pressing it into all the corners. "I imagine not."

He pressed a kiss to her temple. "Leave all this. We'll collect it in the morning before we head topside. Grab anything you think will help you sleep tonight."

"And some food."

He perked up at the mention of sustenance. "You found food?"

Bella motioned at the darkened passageway. "In a box."

He disappeared into the other room, Lunah

trotting after him. Bella set the crate beside the one with the documentation and braced her arm on the top. Leander still sat dejected. A man locked in grief.

"Markus and I are going to sleep near the creek tonight. You're welcome to join us," she said gently.

Sitting back, he looked at his grimy hands. "Do you think maybe I could... I don't know, maybe wash some?"

Bella moved around the table to crouch before him. "I think that would be just fine. There's a waterfall. And the shoreline and creek bed are made of glass pebbles."

He looked up. "Glass?"

"Yes. Markus said there's a beach like it in Ruthenia. It's beautiful. Oberon found it. He drew some pictures and I'm sure he wrote about all the colors."

"I should like to see that, too."

Bella smiled and stood. "Good. It's not too long a walk."

"I'll use the stick Markus found. I did okay helping with...." He cleared his throat when his voice failed. "Helping."

"I'm sorry you lost your friend."

"I don't know what to do now," he whispered, staring at his hands once more. "This is not a crime scene anyone will be able to investigate."

"We investigated," Markus's deep voice said from behind her. "We will be his voice, Mr. Kavont."

Leander glanced up, tears shimmering behind his glasses. "And you will stay even longer to try to find his killer?"

"I don't think we'll have to wait long for his killer to reveal themselves. Once this discovery goes public, their anger won't be contained," Markus said.

Bella nodded. "If what Markus said is true, the crime was one of passion. This discovery upset someone enough to commit murder, hide the location, and attempt to recover anything pertaining to it. But they weren't a criminal, they didn't look hard enough, and when they realize they failed, I agree with Markus, it won't go over well."

Markus hefted his pack over his shoulder. "Come on, before the sun sets completely. I want to make sure we're set up somewhere safe while we can still see to work."

Leander stood and scrubbed a hand over his dusty face. He wobbled until he braced himself on the walking stick. "I'm going to grab some of Oberon's clean clothes to change into."

"Take anything you need," Markus said, squeezing the historian's shoulder on his way past. "We'll wait for you."

Markus picked up a lantern, and Bella followed him down the stairs. Morbid curiosity had her asking, "What did you do for Oberon?"

"Lunah dug a shallow grave in the sand close enough to the body for me to be able to carefully move him. We covered him with sand and then stones. Leander set Oberon's hat on top as an identifying marker. He wants to return at some point with a proper naming stone."

"I hope he gets to do that," Bella said, glancing over her shoulder into the darkness.

Leander hobbled down, the staff clicking on the steps, a bag slung over his shoulder. Odd lumps filled out the bottom. Their small group followed the same path Bella had discovered earlier. The transition from darkness into a semblance of light was easier with the sun weak in the sky. A golden hue illuminated the cavern, the glass water's edge subdued yet no less stunning, the colors vibrant in the soft glow.

"Oh, my stars," Leander said behind them. He stumbled past, the bag sliding off his shoulder to land forgotten amongst the ivy and ferns. Spinning in a slow circle, he looked up, eyes wide. "Oh... my... stars."

Leander splashed into the water, sitting right in the center of the stream. The walking stick bobbed in the water and floated away. Lunah barked and bounced past him, grabbing the makeshift cane between her teeth. He lifted a handful of dripping glass stones, the shimmering crystalline orbs dancing in his palm. "This place is a gift. A beautiful gift from our ancestors. Who... who would want to hide such a remarkable discovery from the rest of the world?"

Markus crouched at the edge of the creek. "That is what we're going to find out, Mr. Kavont."

BEFORE THE SUN ROSE, Markus and Lunah left a sleeping Bella and Leander to search for an easier exit. Whoever had murdered the archaeologist hadn't left the way Oberon at one point had climbed down, though Markus had no doubt Bella's tumble was the original way the location had been found. Climbing a rope required immense physical strength. If Markus wanted to get his wife out of the underground, he'd have to find the secret exit.

Can you scent Oberon? Markus asked along their bond.

She padded ahead, her nose to the sand. *Familiar, not Oberon, but the scent is familiar.*

A lantern cut a wide arc of light through the darkness and Markus held it up higher. *Familiar how?*

Following us, who has been following us.

Alarmed, Markus paused mid-step. *Is the scent old?*

Yes, old as the dead man's scent, yes.

Relief sagged his shoulders and he sighed. *Very good. Ursla'viti.*

She obeyed his command to follow, alternating between the ground and the open air to trail the scent left by the killer. They wove through tight corridors slick with algae. Markus frowned, wondering how in the inhabited world the murderer had found the way.

Sometime later, they emerged into a valley of some sort, the rising sun just beginning to illuminate the sky to a twilight gray. Markus took a moment to ensure the exit was safe. Lunah scouted around and found nothing suspicious. Turning, he took in the opening, which looked to be nothing more than slabs of limestone stacked together at an angle with the sloped opening high enough on the left for him to squeeze through. Ivy dangled over the ledge and ferns sprang from the uneven crevices and along the ground. So different from the desert that he figured was only a short walk away. The colorful birds from the waterfall flew in swooping arcs across the sky, their song the only noise in the quiet dawn.

The return trip to the creek was faster, Lunah leading the way. The two of them were waiting near the opening. Droplets of moisture in the air and on plants sparkled in the faint glow of dawn piercing through the holes above. Markus took a moment to appreciate Bella's beauty surrounded by such wonder. Stars above, how he loved her.

She smiled, a sweet, almost shy upward curl of her lips that contrasted with the woman who'd seduced him so thoroughly yesterday morning. The stolen moment felt like a lifetime ago. They hadn't been given much opportunity to indulge in the deeper intimacy of their relationship. *He* hadn't had the time to deal with how her desire to please him messed with his perception of what happened between mates. Prior to her, expectations were solely on him. If he could please a woman, she *might* decide he was worthy and give him the honor of bonding and carrying the future generation.

Bella hadn't even known what kind of lover he'd be for her. She'd simply accepted and bonded with him because.... Well, he didn't know. They'd never discussed the why of their relationship. The bond had been forged and he'd accepted the outcome. Accepted her. The unmitigated trust she'd placed in him with her bond had begun the journey of him falling for her. Everything after only added to his growing love. Of course, none of his ponderings were appropriate given their situation, and he shook his head and motioned at the dark exit.

"I found the way out," he said.

Leander hoisted his pack onto his shoulder and leaned his weight onto the cane. He pushed his glasses up on his nose. "We must get Oberon's studies first."

"I haven't forgotten." Markus reached for Bella and she stepped over moss-coated rocks to place her hand in his. The connection brought an immediate sense of rightness, the anxiety over their unconventional bond disintegrating at her touch.

"Is the way dangerous?" she asked, her fingers squeezing around his.

He shook his head and kissed her hand.

Tilting her head, she regarded him, her brows drawn. "All right."

Markus didn't know whether to be thankful or disappointed she didn't inquire further about what she must have felt along their bond. Since she was learning all the nuances of their relationship just like him, and he didn't want to explain himself with an audience, he opted for thankful.

Using lanterns, they returned to Oberon's base of operations, collected what Bella had sorted, and then Markus guided them through the twisting rock corridors. The light bounced off the damp walls and slick floor. Rocks skittered from their shoes. Lunah's claws clicked on the stone ground. The lack of conversation and other sounds grated on Markus in a way it hadn't when he'd been alone. Despite the horror of Oberon's death, no one seemed ready or happy to leave the underground. In essence, he was a killjoy for leading them away from the wonderland. The corridor opened into a wider space, the hole of light at the exit a faint glow in the distance.

"Whoa," Bella said, breaking from the line they'd naturally formed. She held the lantern high, the light spilling a wide circle around her. "Look at this."

Lunah went to her side, looking over her shoulder at Markus, her tongue hanging free. Her ears were alert, twitching to the occasional echo of water dropping somewhere in the vast space. Markus set the crate he'd been carrying down and joined them. Brushing his hand between Bella's shoulders he squinted into the darkness.

"What do you see?" he asked softly.

She slid her arm out in a wide arc. "All the lines. Look at them."

Markus blinked, straining to see what she did. Closing his eyes, he followed his bond to Lunah and viewed the cavity from the wolf's perspective. White stripes lined the ground, even dotted with algae and cracked, the symmetry of them was unmistakable. Markus returned to his own sight, able to make out the faint glow of white paint.

Leander stopped on his left. "What is it? I don't see anything."

Bella went deeper, stopping at the first visible line. "It's just like the vertical cemetery from

Oberon's research drawings. His theory of a parking structure. I think… I bet this was a parking area of some sort. The lines are exactly the same."

Markus took Bella's lamp and went to the closest stripe. He knelt and touched the textured paint. He pointed. "Look at this, the light reflects off it."

She rested her hand on his shoulder and crouched. "It's glittery. How odd, I wonder why?"

Markus shrugged and pulled his knife from behind his back. After a detailed search, he found a chunk breaking free from the ground and carefully used the tip of his knife to dislodge it the rest of the way. He held the course section on his palm out to his bride. The smile she bestowed upon him made him feel like he offered her diamonds instead of a painted hunk of rock. And perhaps he did. What made the paint shimmer?

"They won't be able to deny this," Markus said.

Bella took the block, needing both hands. The weight took her by surprise and she nearly dropped it, bracing the mass on her thigh. "I hope he wrote about what he saw since his drawing didn't reveal how the lines looked, only that they existed. If he described it? No, they won't be able to deny the pre-cataclysm connection."

Leander walked over several of the lines. "He had to have seen this. He must have been—" His voice cracked and he covered his mouth for a moment. "So excited. To not be able to share his discovery and the accurate results of his hypothesis? Not fair."

Markus stood. "Murder is rarely fair."

Leander sniffled and looked around. "No, I suppose not."

Bella handed the artifact to Markus before rising. She went to the grieving man and touched his sleeve. "You're his voice now. You'll be the one to bring all his visions, all his dreams, to life."

Lifting his chin, Leander straightened his shoulders and nodded. "Yes, you're right. Do you suppose we have to fear someone silencing us now?"

Lunah growled. The same fierce need to protect coursed through Markus. "Not a concern."

Leander blinked behind his glasses. "Why ever not?"

Markus sank his fingers into the thick, risen fur between Lunah's shoulders. "Because they won't succeed."

CHAPTER

ELEVEN

N EEDING REST, AND A REAL SHOWER, M ARKUS managed to convince Leander to wait a day before they informed the authorities and the Institute of Culture about Oberon's death. Morning's light had brought a welcome sensual experience. His mate's curious touch, and heated responses, had led to another morning of intimate pleasure. He loved the way she demanded he love her hard, a little rough, the way he preferred sex. But, as he watched her dress for the day, he knew when the insatiable newness of their relationship wore off, he wanted to know what slow would feel like with her.

"What is that smile for?" she asked, affixing the leather bracer he'd given her months ago to her left wrist. A false promise band to trick a bad man in her life that had turned into the real thing. A true twist of fate.

He finished tying the leather strand around the end of his braid. "I was contemplating."

"What about?"

Tossing the braid over his shoulder, he

crossed the space between them. He laced his fingers through her left hand. Brushing the bracer with his free hand, he caressed a gentle path up her arm to her throat, where he stroked her thrumming pulse. "I was contemplating slow."

Her brows furrowed. "Slow?"

Leaning in close, he allowed his desire free reign and whispered into her ear, "Over you, behind you, maybe even beneath you, I don't care, but however you want it, I'll be sliding in and out of you slowly."

The hitch of her breath and the heat along their bond made him smile.

"Sound like something you'd want to try?" he asked, trailing his finger to her collarbone.

"Just start slow?"

"All of it. The whole time."

She swallowed, her throat working beneath the pressure of his touch. "What if I don't like it?"

He leaned even closer and kissed the rapid flutter of her pulse. "What if you do?"

Her panting breaths whispered along his jaw, and she grabbed at the front of his shirt. "Oh, summer sun..." she moaned.

"*Dak?*"

"When?"

He opened his mouth to growl *now*, because really? How could he make either of them wait with the arousal flaring between them? But a heavy knock stole the moment. How very typical. Straightening, he glared at the door. Bella dropped her head to his chest, her hand moving low to caress the erection straining his pants. His hips jerked in reaction and he clenched his jaw at the pleasure of her touch, even through the fabric.

"Something will need to be done about this," she murmured. Rising on her tiptoes, she inhaled at his throat. "I can—"

He twisted away from her and pulled his shirt out to cover the evidence of his desire. "I'll be fine."

She didn't speak, but then again, she didn't need to. The disappointment along their bond pierced him like a dagger, made worse by the knowledge only the strongest of her emotions could filter to him. He ignored the discomfort and went to the door, yanking it open. Leander yanked his fist back and blinked.

"Good morning," he said, clasping his hands and dropping them. "I was hopeful you'd be prepared to go to the Institute this morning?"

He glanced over his shoulder. Bella had shouldered her bag and held a crate. Lunah sat next to her, her ears back, tail flicking. She was displeased with him, too. Wonderful. "Yes. Do you have the other crate?"

They'd decided it was safer for each of them to have half the evidence. Just in case. Leander leaned to the left and hoisted up the box. A nod sent his curls bouncing. Markus stepped back and held the door for his females. He took the evidence from Bella as she walked by, and she closed the door behind him. Idly, he wondered if their intimate life would be so easy someday. A smooth give and take where no words would be necessary and awkwardness wouldn't matter.

He shifted the box to one arm and grasped

her elbow as she went to follow Leander. "I'm sorry."

Her beautiful eyes widened and she stepped close enough for her delicious berry and vanilla scent to fill the remaining space between them. "What for?"

"I'm trying to learn," he motioned between them, "this. Us."

Smiling, she rose on her tiptoes and pressed a kiss to his lips. "Me too. We'll figure it out when we aren't being interrupted at every moment."

He laughed and pulled her into his side with his free arm, hugging her tight. He kissed the top of her head. "Won't that be nice?"

She puffed out an extended sigh. "Very."

"Oh, where did you go? Did I lose you both?" Leander called from the stairs.

Bella chuckled and shook her head. "No, we're right behind you."

Markus grasped her hand and laced their fingers together. He leaned close to keep their conversation private as they reached the stairs. "Did I tell you the same scent Lunah caught while following us was preserved outside where we exited?"

He had to keep her moving when she jerked and almost stopped. "No."

"She's going to alert when she scents the person at the Institute."

Bella glanced at him before watching the steps. "You're certain they'll be there?"

"Yes. Oberon knew his attacker. Had brought them to the site. I'm positive of it."

"And you don't want Leander to know?" she whispered at the bottom of the stairs.

"I don't want him to give anything away. The person thinks they've gotten away with murder. Even if we show up with a box of theories and artifacts, they'll think they're safe. I don't want them to believe otherwise."

"Lunah won't be enough, not for these people. They don't understand how your bond works. I barely do."

Markus nodded and squeezed her hand. "I know. But with her being aware of the person's scent, it'll make it easier to find the proper evidence." He leaned in and placed a gentle kiss on her lips, whispering, "I have done this a time or two in other countries. Trust me?"

A flush bloomed across her cheeks. "I do."

He gave her hand another squeeze before releasing. "You'll get used to Lunah being part of our process as we work more together."

Outside, the cool morning air teased his braid and fluttered his shirt. Leander marched across the street, shoulders back, head high. A man on a mission. Bella hurried after him, touching his sleeve once she caught him. The historian smiled, his face relaxing in relief.

The wolf did a full body shake and gave a quiet woof. Her golden eyes gleamed in the bright light.

Tell me if you scent anyone familiar on the walk, Markus instructed, following behind the small group.

The wolf did a full body shake and gave a

quiet woof. Her golden eyes gleamed in the bright light.

He shifted the crate to both arms. No one bothered them or tried to inquire about what they carried. Whatever Thanzia's standards of laws were, they kept people in line. So far, the situation with Oberon was the only hint of wrongdoing in the city. No thieves disrupted businesses. No fights broke out among customers in shops. Neighbors did not violently quarrel. The near non-existent crime made him wonder at the punishment. Even his beloved homeland had its share of issues. Then again, you couldn't have a country full of alpha dominant personalities and be completely peaceful.

The impressive gates of the Institute of Culture came into view. Sun dappled through the gently swaying tree limbs high above. Despite the cheery song of birds and clear blue sky, the gathering of buildings loomed in ominous silence, their shadows cold. As if the very stone mourned the loss of one of its own within the walls.

Leander hesitated at the steps to the Museum of History, then he took a bracing step forward, nodding in thanks to Bella, who opened the tall door. This time, Lunah came in with them. She lifted her snout into the air, her nostrils flaring. The door closed behind Markus and he followed Leander to the west wing.

The person is here, the person is.

By the sudden tension in Bella's shoulders, Markus knew Lunah had spoken to them both.

Can you tell which direction they went? Markus asked.

Everywhere, I scent the person everywhere.

The space bustled with academics, visitors, and clerks, all carrying themselves in slightly different ways. Visitors lingered, taking in subtle nuances that had become common sights to those who worked in the building. Academics were immersed in whatever book, artifact, or research paper they carried, as though it had to be solved or learned with expedience. The clerks paid no attention to either, hurrying from one point to another, easily avoiding bystanders. None of them paid their little group any mind. No eyes lingered. No one rushed off to go unnoticed. Yet, the killer *had* been through here. Today.

They made their way to the second floor of the west wing. Leander guided them to a large conference room. Tall windows overlooked a manicured ground, and beyond in the vast distance of the desert, a vertical cemetery broke up the endless sand and boulders. Not the one they'd visited, but another that served the city and perhaps the inhabitants of the next closest town.

Markus set his box on the elongated wooden table. The unpolished, natural planks had soaked up all the mistakes over what appeared to be decades. Spilt ink. Grease marks. Heat circles. Smudged paint and other unidentifiable stains. Framed rough sketches of early Thanzian life filled the walls. Bella inspected them, her fingers brushing the occasional frame but stopping at touching the paper within.

A man and woman rushed through the doors, colorful streams of fabric fluttering behind them. The man's a shade of blue and vivid green around his waist, the woman's teal and rich purple around her left upper arm. They both touched a hand to their chest before Leander, who returned the gesture. They then pivoted toward Markus and Bella, doing the same.

"We welcome you to our space." The woman's bright orange tunic gown with gold embroidery along the hem and sleeves complimented her rich brown skin. Her dark eyes were both curious and solemn. "May we learn of what discovery you made?"

Leander spoke in their native language. The man wove on his feet and clutched at his pale gray shirt, his arm a dark contrast across the fabric. He spoke rapidly and the woman cut in, waving her hand around. Leander shook his head and made *calm-down* motions. When they'd both calmed down enough, he spoke again. The woman covered her mouth over a jagged cry and turned her back to the room. The man collapsed into the nearest chair. Leander swiped both hands under his glasses.

Leander attempted to speak, pressed a hand to his upper chest, and tried again. "I introduce Dm'evlo kwan Con'diaye," he motioned to the man holding his head in his hand on the table. "He worked closely with Oberon, helping him catalog his research and write proposals for getting his artifacts in the museums here and across the inhabited world. And this—" He stepped closer to the woman, who raised a trembling hand but didn't turn around. "Is S'arbi ni kwan Aliounyse. She's the director of archaeology."

"We wish we had better news to deliver," Markus said.

"He is..." S'arbi's voice cracked and she audibly sniffled. "He is in the ground. A grave for the shamed, the unworthy of recognition for generations, by generations."

"That is not true," Bella rushed forward and touched the woman on the shoulder. "He can be moved, or he can remain among his greatest discovery. You may bring recognition to him in that place, which will always be known for him and him alone. He can be honored in your history forever."

"Is it so great? What he found?" S'arbi asked, turning, tears streaking her dark cheeks.

Markus reached for his box. "Here, let us show you."

ARTIFACTS COVERED the entire table in the conference room. Bella stood back and wished the weight on her heart would lift, but she figured until they brought justice to Oberon, the sensation would remain. The sadness of his closest colleagues lessened the excitement of a once-in-a-lifetime discovery. They spoke quietly, inspecting each item, reading each paper, with a longing to have their friend explain it to them. Which he would never do.

Leander sat with his hands steepled at the farthest end of the table. "Is there anyone you can think of who would wish Oberon's finds to be kept secret?"

Dm'evlo held several drawings in both hands, passing them over and behind each other. "Since no one has come forward to offer a claim? No, I cannot imagine anyone being upset enough to kill over the discovery."

"I agree," S'arbi said, inspecting a handful of glass pebbles on her palm. "These were truly from a creek bed?"

Bella nodded. "With a waterfall."

"Amazing." The little rocks scattered on the wood as she gently poured them from her hand back to the table. "If someone had attempted to say the site was their find, we would suspect. But no one has said anything. Oberon's disappearance was a mystery to everyone in this building and the entire Institute."

"We need to take the information to the proper authorities and allow them to open an investigation," Markus said.

Dm'evlo shook his head. "I do not believe we do not investigate like you. We, as the victims, must present the crime and the suspect. If the evidence is enough, the verdict will be given and justice served."

"Will you continue to search?" S'arbi asked, her gaze pleading.

Sympathy twisted inside Bella. "Of course we will." Annoyance flared along her bond with Markus and she turned to look at him. "Right?"

"*Dak.*"

Thank you, she mouthed before turning back to S'arbi. "His office was in too much disarray for us to get anything useful. Did he have a secondary work space that might have fared better?"

Dm'evlo nodded, rising. "He did. We shared the room and no one has been there since his disappearance, except for me. It will please me to take you."

The items were repackaged and S'arbi and Leander left to place them in a secure location. Dm'evlo led them downstairs and across the foyer to large glass double doors set into stone. Words in Thanzian were chiseled over the threshold. Patrons milled about in the brightly lit area, looking over stations, artifacts and listening to what Bella assumed were historians giving guided tours. Dm'evlo held one of the doors for them.

"Oh, I am apologizing, the animal is not allowed in this space," he said, frowning, his attention on Lunah.

Markus smiled in understanding. "No problem." Bella took a step to follow and Markus shook his head. "Go on, I'll find you."

Bella offered Dm'evlo a smile. "Can you wait for me for just a moment?"

"I will," he said like a vow, pressing a hand to his chest.

"Thank you." Bella felt compelled to repeat the gesture. The smile he beamed said she'd made the right decision.

She hurried after Markus, grasping his sleeve. "What did Lunah say?" When he continued walking, looking around, Bella moved closer. "I felt your anticipation."

He glanced at her and opened the door. "She

scented the person following us. They went into the museum. I'm having her go around the building and find a back exit that they've used or is used often, and wait. If we find the suspect, they may try to run."

"That's why you didn't mind sending her out."

"Having her with us would be easiest. She'd make a positive identification on sight, but this works, too. She'll know the moment they escape and can subdue, if necessary." He ruffled her ears, and off she went, her feet kicking up leaves and dead grass on her way around the building. He laced their hands together. "I didn't mean to exclude you. I figured you'd be ready to see Oberon's workspace. At least one that hasn't been destroyed."

"I am," she agreed. "But I'm more eager to find the person responsible for the destroying."

He rolled one shoulder. "Can't argue against that."

Dm'evlo grinned when he spotted them, his teeth bright against his dark skin, and motioned for them to come along, still holding the door open with his back. Leander and S'arbi were crossing the foyer, and they increased their steps.

"I will locate P'tir and Ta'neesh if you will take them to your office?" S'arbi said, her hands clasped behind her back.

Dm'evlo nodded. "That is well. Perhaps locate Director I'sa?"

"I believe I'sa had a meeting today, but I will ask."

S'arbi went to the left as Dm'evlo led them to

the right. Bella wanted to stop and look at everything, but Dm'evlo kept a clipped, familiar pace. He guided them around pedestals, and cases, through two different cultures, and into a back corridor. Unlike the wood-paneled walls and bright window lit spaces of the west wing, this corridor was nothing but white. White stone floor. White painted cement brick walls. White ceiling. Glass-covered wall sconces bounced light around the long passage. Dm'evlo's shoes squeaked on the tile. He pulled a key from a strand around his neck as they turned a corner and came to a door on the left. The lock released, and he pushed the door open.

"Here is the office we shared. Oberon Rima's desk is on the left, mine is on the right. You are welcome to search through anything in this space," Dm'evlo said, stepping aside once they entered the room after he lit lanterns.

Floor-to-ceiling shelving units formed shallow rows and made her think of the job she'd left behind. Boxes, envelopes, files, and objects enclosed in glass took up every inch of free space. The rows were barely large enough to squeeze through to the other side of the room where the duo had their desks. Markus had to twist sideways and inch through.

"Did he bring anything from the excavation site here, do you know?" Markus asked.

Shelves rustled several rows over and Dm'evlo's voice floated to them. "Oh, I am not certain? If so, he would have kept them in one of his drawers. He is... was... very detailed before allowing me to catalog anything new to display or archive."

Bella went around the desk and sat in the worn leather chair. She lit the desk lamp and then took in the cluttered station. Unlike his office, which had been professional as far as she'd been able to tell, this space was cluttered. Evidence of hours spent researching, immersed in the love of a career. She rested her hands on her lap. Dm'evlo pressed a hand to his chest, the other to the desk, closed his eyes and muttered soft words in his native tongue.

Out of respect, Bella waited until he finished before sifting through the layers of paper. The edges of a black rock peeked out from under a book, laying askew against a small, rectangular box. Bella used her index fingers to pull it forward without disturbing the precarious arrangement of objects all around the chunk. The white, shimmery paint was immediately recognizable.

She straightened in excitement, her head whipping around to search for her husband. "Markus, look!"

Dm'evlo leaned over the desk, his brows raised. "That is like the one you brought back."

"Exactly the same, just longer," Markus confirmed, setting down a stack of familiar flat cards wrapped in cord. "Where did these come from?"

"Another site he helped excavate in northern Thanzia," Dm'evlo said. "About eight months ago, I believe. We have similar ones on display in the museum from all over the inhabited world."

"But none from here?" Bella asked.

Dm'evlo shook his head. "No, and no one believed he truly found them from here. The site is on the border with Cairo, you understand."

Bella met Markus's somber stare. "He found dozens in the underground ruins," Bella whispered.

"No denying where those came from," Markus said.

Dm'evlo took an unsteady step away. "I-I did not even recognize them until right now. Those," he pointed, "were among the many things from where he died?"

Markus nodded. "Yes. And I suspect in many of these boxes, we'll find artifacts Oberon had been quietly collecting from across the inhabited world with the hopes of proving his theory correct about a prior civilization in Thanzia."

"Nonsense!" a female voice echoed from behind them. A tall woman appeared from between shelving units. Her family colors of moss green and creamy pink fell in graceful waves from her left upper arm to her knee. The low lighting enhanced her pale brown skin. Ribbons in her family colors were woven into tiny braids that fell past her shoulders. "Utter nonsense. Thanzia was established as a completely new land six hundred years ago."

Dm'evlo pressed a hand to his chest. "Ta-neesh, welcome to my space."

Ta-neesh's light brown eyes flashed, yet she returned the gesture. "I thank you for the welcome, Dm'evlo. Now, onto this... this falsehood."

"I am apologizing," Dm'evlo began, "but is it a falsehood when the evidence is showing we were not the first ones in this land?"

A man appeared behind Ta-neesh, S'arbi inching past behind him, her face pinched. The man held his head up, the light shining off his ebony head. Berry red, pale yellow, and dark yellow fabric were wrapped around his thin waist and fluttered near his ankle from his left hip.

Dm'evlo pressed a hand to his chest. "P'tir, welcome to my space."

P'tir ignored the welcome, his dark gaze fixed on Bella and the few contents on the desk that weren't papers. He pointed. "Those things are lies. Each of them."

Markus raised a brow and stepped close, until his hip brushed her shoulder. "Lies? How so?"

Leander stepped from between shelves to stand beside S'arbi, adjusting his glasses on his nose. "Yes, how so? I was present when we collected the findings Oberon himself discovered in the underground cavern."

P'tir crossed his arms over his chest, pulling his dark orange shirt tight across his shoulders. "Then he placed them there in hopes of fooling the citizens of a lie he could not release for his own ambitions."

"I must agree with P'tir," Ta'neesh said. "Centuries of exploration of our lands has yielded no proof of a previous civilization. Then Oberon stumbles across some a few miles from here, and we are to believe everything we know of our land is false? I think not."

Bella pushed the rock closer to Ta'neesh. "No one is trying to take away the accomplishments or history of your people. What Oberon believed may reveal why certain traditions are so important. Where they came from. Where *you*, your ancestors, truly came from. Who wouldn't want to learn such things?"

Ta'neesh picked up the rock. "This is from the ground?"

"Yes. It's the same paint that's found in the first vertical cemetery," Bella said.

"In Akurdin," Leander offered, moving closer to the desk. "Oberon has many notes and drawings, and this find—" Leander pressed his index finger to the rock. "—is key evidence to his theories being proven."

S'abri spoke in low tones in Thanzian. Ta'neesh and P'tir turned to face her. Ta'neesh's shoulders tightened while P'tir's fists clenched. S'abri held her hands open, she pointed at her palm and then motioned around herself. Dm'evlo and Leander joined the conversation. Wondering if they were discussing the evidence or the legitimacy of said artifacts, Bella braced her elbows on the desk and her chin on her palms.

The discussion soon turned heated. Leander marched to the nearest shelving unit, stomped his foot, and pointed, nearly shouting. Ta'neesh moved closer to him, touching a hand to his shoulder. P'tir shook his head and sliced a hand through the air. S'arbi's words turned pleading.

"Wish I knew this language," Markus muttered. "I wonder who's winning the debate."

"Oberon's evidence, I think," Bella said.

Leander pointed a finger at P'tir, his words harsh. P'tir recoiled and then threw up his hands and stomped off. Leander and Ta'neesh spoke quietly and then Leander looked at Bella and Markus.

"We're going upstairs to review the findings we brought back. Please bring any objects you discover that are the same," Leander stated before turning on his heel and stalking after P'tir. Ta'neesh hurried after, her family colors fluttering in her wake.

Dm'evlo and S'arbi looked at each other and spoke. Nodding, Dm'evlo faced the desk. "I am going to help in the search if this is acceptable?"

Bella stood. "Of course. You know this space better than anyone and you saw what we returned with. Did anything look familiar?"

"Many things," Dm'evlo said, eyes wide.

"I wish to help," S'arbi said. "Leander can handle those two for a short time."

Bella glanced at Markus, anxiety tightening her chest. "Not if one of them is a killer."

TWELVE

"ARE YOU GOING TO CALL LUNAH?"

Markus looked at Bella and shook his head, following a few steps behind Dm'evlo and S'arbi. "It'd take too long to go to the door she's nearest. She'll remain outside and be there if we need her."

His wolf much preferred the outdoors to having to behave herself inside. He had no doubt she'd stuffed her nose in some animal burrow and had found a place to dig where no one would notice.

Dm'evlo carried a wicker basket overflowing with treasures. He and S'arbi spoke in low tones, their worry a tangible thing between them. All four of them had worked at a fevered pace to fill the basket with recognizable objects, not wanting Leander to be alone with the evidence for long, which could place the historian in danger. Anticipation thrummed through Markus. A sense of the inevitable end arriving.

Upstairs, in the same conference room from earlier, Leander stood with the boxes before him.

Several items were laid out and he was pulling another free as they walked in, explaining where they'd found the object. Ta'neesh held one of the small, flat rectangles with black cracked glass on the front and silver metal on the back. Dm'evlo quickly set the basket down, dug around inside, and pulled out a similar object, only instead of a silver back, this one had blue metal. The two closed the distance and compared the item, pointing out the subtle differences in an otherwise identical item. P'tir stood near the windows, nibbling on his thumb.

S'arbi joined the excited duo, adding her own comparisons. A disk with painting on one side and reflective on the other. Leander handed several more to her, all with different works of art. The historians couldn't help trying to guess what they must have been.

"Perhaps they hung from windows?" Ta'neesh surmised, rounding the desk with one in hand and holding it closer to the natural light source. "Watch how the light bounces and reflects like a prism. If they spun, they would have art on one side and a prism on the other."

Leander joined her, one in hand, mimicking her holding the reflective side toward the light. A rainbow line danced across the opposite wall. "Astonishing. I think you may be correct. These are other items that have been found around the world. To believe each culture, no matter the language must have decorated their house in similar manners..." He shook his head in wonder. "A commonality across our entire race."

"So many common items found in every

country," Dm'evlo said, setting like objects beside the ones Leander had unboxed. "We must read Oberon's theory concerning our past. I do not believe we can afford to ignore the proo—"

"This is not proof!" P'tir exploded from his place near the window, snatching a disk from Ta'neesh and throwing it across the room. "There is no confirmation here! Only a man so desperate to see his name in our history he planted all these *things* in a cave full of... of odd rock formations and dared to call them artifacts of Thanzia!"

Bella stepped forward but thankfully kept her distance from the angry curator. "They were not odd rock formations. They're remnants of buildings. Even vehicles were down there."

"Absurd!" P'tir fumed, color rising high on his cheeks. "Anything you thought you saw down there was nothing more than light playing tricks. It's so dark, not even a lamp illuminated anything worth looking at."

P'tir stepped to the desk and swiped a hand through the ancient objects, sending them flying and skittering in every direction. Markus yanked Bella into his chest as a chunk of broken green glass flew by and shattered against the wall.

"All of this rubbish is just that. Trash. Garbage. *Not* our history!"

Dm'evlo inched around the table. "I disagree, curator. Oberon left all the objects he'd collected from other sites in the inhabited world in our office. He certainly didn't cart dozens and dozens of artifacts from our very museum. That level of theft—"

"Everyone would have noticed." Ta'neesh interrupted. "He would have needed to steal from our exhibits to amass such a collection." She released a long sigh and picked up one of the pebbles that had been scattered in P'tir's fit. "I think, as much as it pains me to say, we will need to hold an Institute meeting. Oberon's site, these findings, it all must be further explored. We need to reach out to other museums who have helped excavate similar sites. We need—"

"We need *nothing*!" P'tir screamed. He went to reach for the nearest box and both Leander and Dm'evlo grabbed an arm. The man bucked and yanked, but the two historians held tight. "Let me go, you idiots! Even from the dead, Oberon is attempting to erase our great heritage. I stopped him! I prevented a terrible mistake from being made! And now you are wanting to let it happen anyway?"

A shocked stillness filled the room.

P'tir seemed to realize his confession, halting mid-yank to stare in dismay at everyone looking at him with mixed emotions. Anger filled Dm'evlo's stare and clenched his jaw. Leander released P'tir as though he'd been burned. Tears tracked down S'arbi's cheeks. Disbelief and revulsion twisted Ta'neesh's face.

"Tell us you did not," S'arbi demanded. "Tell us it was not you who stole so much from Oberon!"

"S-stole?" P'tir sputtered. "Stole? Me? I tried to protect our nation! Oberon and his absurd theories are a danger."

"A danger to what?" Ta'neesh demanded. "Your misguided loyalty to a group of nomads who founded our nation hundreds of years ago? They had no way to tell us where they came from, P'tir. That is up to us to learn by what they left behind. So, we discover we may have had ancestors prior to the cataclysm. Why would that be so horrible to you?"

"We are a pure and noble people. We are..." P'tir's voice cracked. "We are of this land... I just..." He looked down at his hands, stumbling backward.

"What did you do, P'tir?" Dm'evlo asked in a sad, quiet tone, maintaining a hold on the now trembling man.

Still looking at his hands, P'tir muttered, "No one could know. No one could see. Had to... protect us. Keep it all a secret. Had to..."

S'arbi covered her mouth and turned her back to everyone, her shoulders shaking. Ta'neesh sat on the floor, her family colors pooling around her legs.

Leander took hold of P'tir. "Dm'evlo, if you would please do the honors of gathering your law enforcement?"

Dm'evlo blinked and yanked his hand from P'tir. "I will go now, yes."

Markus released the hold he'd had on Bella during the drama. "Will you let my wolf in, please?"

Dm'evlo nodded and then hurried from the room.

A man is going to let you in at the front. Follow my scent back to the room on the second floor, Markus told Lunah.

Yes, alpha, yes.

Markus went to the door and waited. Her beautiful silver form appeared down the hall, golden eyes alert, ears pointed forward. The moment she reached the door, he said across their bond, *Is the scent from the cave in this room?*

She padded forward, nose in the air. P'tir recoiled at the sight of her. *Yes, the scent, yes.*

Bella raised her brows and Markus nodded. *Walk to the scent.*

She obeyed, going to P'tir and sitting. "*Dokhor vok,* Lunah."

Happiness glowed in her eyes at the praise.

Markus met Bella's stare. "We have him."

EPILOGUE

HAVEN CITY, SZIVERIA
Two weeks later...

CHAIRS, tables, couches, beds, shelves... anything a house could need was stacked, hung, and wedged into a large, two-story brick building. Bella stared at the chaos and took a deep breath.

"Well," Madeleine said slowly, stepping in behind Markus. "If you two can't find what you're looking for here, Sziveria probably doesn't have it."

He rested his hands on her mother's shoulders. "If *we* can't find. You'll be living there, too."

Madeleine waved away the offer. "I've had my home to decorate. I'm along to watch Bella find something she loves until she sees the price."

"Mother," Bella choked.

"It's true," she said, moving to the nearest chair and flipping over a tag hanging from a thin white cord. "See?"

Bella leaned forward and squinted at the printed price. "Oh, that's just ridiculous. It's a chair, not a throne!"

Madeleine let the tag flutter from her fingertips. "Mm-hmm."

Markus wrapped his arm around her shoulders and hugged her to his chest. "We talked about this. She's not going to touch a tag. Right?"

Bella motioned to the chair. "Had I known the prices would be so high, I would have kept what we had already."

Sighing, Madeleine moved deeper into the shop. "You hated that furniture."

"It functioned."

Fixing her with a pointed stare, Madeleine lifted a brow. "And when Markus has to have an important meeting in our home, what then?"

Bella tried to imagine Markus welcoming some Ruthenian national into their beautiful apartment with their old ratty furniture and shuddered. "Fine, but nothing too expensive."

Markus stopped in front of a large wicker couch with thick padded cushions. The wood painted white, paired with the rich blue fabric, was a beautiful combination. "This is nice."

A love seat and two wing-backed white wicker chairs were with the set. She reached for the tag hanging from the back of the couch. Markus leaped forward faster than she could react and ripped the paper free.

"Nope," he said. "I'll hang on to this to give to the sales clerk. Now, let's go find a dresser."

"But—"

His hand settled on her hip and he urged her

toward a section of the store with dressers arranged so close together there was barely room to walk between them. "No arguing. We made more than enough from the extra time on the Thanzia case."

Sadness swept through Bella. Yes, they'd closed the case, but the reminder of all a man had lost, what his friends had lost, still broke her heart. Markus hugged her close and kissed her temple.

"It's okay, *krahet'sna*," he whispered.

She took a deep breath and urged the emotion to dissipate. For the week-long return voyage back to Sziveria, Markus had suffered right alongside her seasickness. Not in illness but in her negative emotional state. Hopefully, over time, she'd learn to identify the bond as he could. So far, she'd failed, but she was determined.

Madeleine called them from a few rows over. After hours of searching, they'd furnished the living room, the rest of their bedroom, and with limited arguing, a new bedroom set for her mother.

Back at the apartment, a wrapped package was waiting in front of the door. Markus handed the paper-covered box to Bella before unlocking the door. The hefty weight took her by surprise and she needed both arms.

Madeleine leaned over to look. "Who's it from?"

Bella smiled. "Leander Kavont. Who we assisted in Thanzia. He works for the National Museum of Sziveria."

"Oh, I see. Rather large box, wonder what he sent?"

Lunah bounced in front of the door, whining in happiness that her people had returned home. Madeleine showered her with attention, leading her with enthusiastic steps to the kitchen.

"May I see?" Markus asked, reaching for the box.

"Yes, of course." Bella passed him the package and used her foot to close the front door. She followed him to the dining room. An entire room for dining. That she lived in such a large space after so many years in a tiny house still amazed her.

Using his knife, he cut through the paper and opened the box. After a quick look inside, he stepped away, grinning. "For you."

Madeleine joined Markus, peering into the box. "Oh my."

Curious, Bella peered into the box and gasped. She reached in and pulled out a handful of reflective disks, a folder of Oberon's sketches, two carefully wrapped cobalt glass birds, and a glass orb with what appeared to be an ocean wave captured inside. The entire bottom of the box was covered in glass pebbles in every color imaginable.

"Why would he send us all of this?" she asked in wonder, picking up the orb. "These glass sculptures are priceless artifacts from that site."

Opening the file, Markus removed a folded slip of paper. "Perhaps this will tell you."

Bella unfolded the sheet and read aloud, "Dear friends, I cannot begin to describe the wonders Oberon's Falls has revealed to the archaeological team in place. I am only thankful I was allowed to be included. The excavation has not been without peril. We've discovered two areas within the cavern that are unstable. Perhaps in the future, engineers will be able to figure out how to make the areas safe, but for now, they'll keep their secrets.

"The birds and the orb were found during a venture into the ruins where the falls themselves are located. So much glass as though it had been a store, museum, or perhaps a factory of some sort. Certainly provided us with an answer to the mystery of how an entire creek bed formed from glass.

"Ta'neesh had the printing department at the Institute create presses from Oberon's sketches of the falls. They're selling them at the museums to help fund the research of the site and to reveal to the inhabited world what has been discovered here. Ta'neesh wanted you to have the entire collection as a thank you. We all hope you enjoy the history you helped bring to the inhabited world. All my gratitude, Leander."

Bella refolded the letter and took a bracing breath to dissipate the tears.

"That was lovely," Madeleine said softly. She picked up one of the cobalt birds. "These are so similar to our Wintervail birds."

"Yes," Bella said, accepting the folder of prints from Markus. "I think as more and more pre-cataclysm sites are discovered, we will learn many of our traditions started so much earlier than we could imagine."

"Was quitting the SNID basement position worth it, now?" Markus asked, inspecting the frozen wave.

Bella quirked a brow and set down the sketches. Was leaving her basement job beneficial? All the things she'd experienced were because he wouldn't give up on keeping her at his side. She wrapped her arms around his neck and pressed her body close. Rising on her tiptoes to keep her words private, she whispered into his ear, "Should I thank you properly?"

His body tightened against hers. Her feet left the ground and she found herself being carried through the apartment. "Watch Lunah, Madeleine?"

The door to the bedroom closed on her mother's laughter.

9 781955 293211